Clarence,

Now walk it out!

Love
Nicole
H

Broken Pieces
'N Rare Pearls

Broken Pieces
'N Rare Pearls

A Memoir by
NIKKI TOWNES

SEVENHORNS
PUBLISHING

Broken Pieces 'N Rare Pearls, A Memoir by Nikki Townes

Published by Sevenhorns Publishing
A Division of SevenHorns, LLC
276 5th Avenue, Suite 704
New York, NY 10001
www.sevenhornspublishing.com

Publishing Support: Ari Rosoff

Design: Branded Human

Visit the author's website at www.NikkiTownesBooks.com.

Library of Congress Control Number: 2018952226

ISBN 978-1-7323870-6-5 (hc)

Manufactured in the United States of America.

In memory of the deceased:

To my Uncle George, who charged me to build bridges,
to my Great-Grandfather, Pop, who put a pencil in my six-year-old
hand and told me to write my story,
to my Grandmothers, whose broken pieces became my rare pearls,
and to Mr. Dick Gregory, my neighbor, who died while I was writing
this book.

Your living was not in vain.

Foreword

The objective of this book is to come clean with God. The only way that we can do that is to dedicate a time in our lives when nothing else is more important than being honest. Before coming to God in honesty, we need to come to ourselves. My mom once said to me, "If you can't be honest with anyone else, at least be honest with yourself." This was good counsel.

The paradox, of course, is that it is impossible to truly come to yourself without God's assistance. So then we are in a quandary, and *this* is why it is necessary to send souls out into the world that can assist in the salvation process. I cannot save you, but I can show you how to be saved. I cannot be honest for you, but I can be honest with you and teach you how to be honest with yourself.

Take one year; dedicate that time as a season in your life wherein you are determined to come to your center—the center of who you are, the core of your being. In that center, there is a great pool; there is a peace, an inner understanding, a tank of readiness to change into whosoever God needs you to be so that someone else might be saved. Read, meditate, learn, and write your way out of the lie and into the truth. Submit yourself to reading the weekly portion that I provide for you in the back of this book. Even when it is laborious, plow through it. Journal daily, even when you think you have nothing to say. Commit to keeping this rhythm until you come to the end. Like penicillin, I don't know exactly how God's supernatural power works, but I can always investigate it later, once the ear infection is gone.

When all other voices came crashing in, forcing themselves against the gates of my holy of holies, my inner soul, it was the life practice of reading the Torah annually, and then the whole bible as an obligation, that protected me from bad counsel. Not that I didn't make bad decisions, but demonic decisions were not made for me. I participated in my own way out, and then back in, to my core.

Once you know your way to the tree of life, you'll never go thirsty for other waters again.

Prologue

Without blood there is no remission of sins. Without the remission of sins, you are not forgiven. Without forgiveness, you are locked out of the tree of life. Without the tree of life, you die. The wages of sin is death; but the gift of God is eternal life. For God so loved the world that He gave His only begotten son, that whosoever believes in Him will not perish, but have everlasting life. If you believe in God, you are entitled to the blood of Jesus Christ. The desire is to access the blood of Jesus. The only way to obtain the blood of Jesus is through a blood transfusion. Jesus has to give His blood, and you have to receive it as your own. You cannot reject the blood of Jesus Christ if you want to live. The ultimate goal is to accept the blood of Jesus. The only way to accept Jesus' blood is to accept His instructions.

This is hard work.

Today, I grieve.
Tomorrow, there's sh*t to do.

Part One
Old Things Are Passed Away

CHAPTER ONE

Whol "*E*" Ness Altars Everything

White Sheets

I give myself permission to grieve today: to wallow over disappointments, lost chances, missed opportunities, grave failures, and casualties I could have prevented or I chose to be the victim of. I give myself permission to mourn the life I should have had, filled with adventure, good health, profound understanding and endless love. I give myself permission to feel deeply the things I'd rather not feel: dreams that will never come true, fantasies that will never surface past nightfall; the good deeds I would have done had I ever amounted to somebody—anybody.

Today, I give myself permission to grieve, 'cuz tomorrow, there's sh*t to do.

It's hard living, walking, breathing with a limp—a constant reminder that the cost of following God means that outside of Him you will never feel certain of anything else again. I mean like, ever. And this isn't a bad thing. It's reality. Most prefer to exist never swallowing the blue pill, but like Neo in The Matrix, did I ever truly have a choice? There was a pounding in me that haunted me day and night, a nagging that was continual, seducing me to wake up, pull back the blinds, set back the curtains, and face the truth: there is a God, and He wants something from me.

And that's where my misery began and begins over and over and over again. Once you realize that God exists and that He is real, living here in this simulation is at best subpar, and at worst, a daily grind. And yet it is His will that we live it. Often I wonder why living here was necessary. I mean, to live here as a drone, what benefit would there be, and to what end, or for what purpose?

There are benefits however in not swallowing the blue pill. Ignorance truly is bliss. Don't let anyone tell you different. Adam didn't notice Eve's cellulite, nor did Eve notice Adam's beer belly, in the garden. Those were the perks of staying in the simulation. Who cares if it's not reality? If you've ever seen *Shallow Hal*, you know what I'm talking about.

I hear banging, talking, and building outside of my window. My daughter died on June 3rd, but I don't want to grieve this year on her birthday. Today I'll grieve instead. I'll blame it on her so that I can compact all of my feelings of grief into one neat little convenient day, as not to take up too much time. A day you can fake; more than that and folks will roll their eyes. But, I need a personal day today. Chances are, I'll still do laundry. Yes, even in the midst of grief, there is still sh*t to do.

Turns out I have a leaky heart valve. I had a heart murmur as a child but it was dismissed as nothing and I'm grateful for that. Perhaps I would have grieved earlier. To me, having a heart murmur is symbolic. It means having a complaint that won't stop. Over time, the complaint in my heart began to pound even louder until the floodgate that is my valve could no longer keep quiet. The complaint turned into discontentment without my knowing it, and it spilled into the spaces in my body, overtaking my ability to circulate blood properly, incapacitating my ability to breathe…to live.

C'Mon, Let's Face It—Ordinary Sucks

"My foot almost slipped when I saw how the wicked prospered and then became righteous." ~ Nikki Townes

I had a heart murmur as a child. It was nothing, I was told, and at the time it was. Except, every night after a sporting practice I felt unusual pain in my legs, and not the kind that stretching can alleviate. I lay on my back, across my bed, with my legs elevated on the wall. I remember this clearly. I remember my room, and I remember thinking that something about this wasn't normal. But I learned to live with it, like everything else. I compensated for the lack of oxygen to my lungs. I overcompensated for the lack of blood and the need for it to be circulating throughout my body, making everything make sense. I learned to live with it. I accepted the fact that I had terrible circulation. Over the years I owned my genes, giving in to the life that was handed down to me. A life without air. A life without blood. It became my home.

Living each day tired, fatigued beyond measure, and imposing a title on yourself that is contrary to your design causes conflict. My mind was telling me one thing. My heart was telling me another. My mind was telling me that I had the capacity for greatness. My heart was telling me that I didn't. And though I was prone to believe my heart, my mind just wouldn't let me. So instead of doing it, I would think about doing it, and try to do it, until my heart would convince my mind of its reality. I didn't have the heart to be extraordinary.

Dirty Waters

I read today that there is a difference between living water and dead water. Dead water collects in our bodies and is useless. Stored, excess water retention. But when the body is starved during a dry fast it finds hidden resources to heal itself, creating water—living water—from within. This shocked me because Jesus spoke of it with the Samaritan woman at the well. Jesus knew about the living water before biologists did.

For some reason, I'm compelled to separate myself again, casting off eating as my stress release. It became my solution to every problem. I used it to procrastinate or soothe. When I'm angry, I have a bad habit of self-destructing; and I'm usually angry with myself, or God, or both.

I try not to be angry with God anymore, which makes it so much harder to take all the blame myself. I wonder if always blaming yourself can cause heart failure. Sometimes blame becomes too much for any one person to handle; yet no one knows. Maybe that's why they call heart attacks the silent killer.

What was I blaming myself for? I was blaming myself for not living up to the standards I set, constantly missing the mark for greatness, and yet being incapable of being ordinary. Not incapable in the way you're thinking. Incapable like lacking the ability to make the good decisions that normal people make, and then harboring in myself the cesspool of dead weight.

Dead weight. What exactly does that mean? Well, in the body it means cells that are sickly, weak, unwilling or unable to fulfill their purpose. They occupy space, but they are dead. During a dry fast the body realizes that it is in crisis, and when in crisis it turns on those who are not getting the job done. Quite simply, the body audits everyone and anything that isn't producing properly. "Sickly" is suddenly sticking out like a sore thumb.

The body becomes dangerously thirsty. Why would being thirsty cause such a surge of productivity, especially if it's harmful? Because thirst causes the body to catch fire to burn what needs to be burned. It's a fire that burns counterfeits, fakes, lies, and liars. The fire burns the dead waters.

A Leaky Heart Valve, Go Figure!

I may have been a hesitator my whole life, by design. I was created that way. That was fine for a time. When it comes to the things of this world, it's better to hesitate. We need to evaluate the things around us and analyze before we make decisions. Not so with God.

With God, the process is completely different. We can't hesitate when it comes to Him because hesitation reveals doubt. You can believe in God (that there is a God) and still fail to believe Him. The result is that to you, He isn't God at all. The epitome of disrespect is to believe in God and yet not believe Him. What you're saying is that you believe that He exists, but He doesn't have any power to do what He says He will do. That's a problem.

Since childhood I've had a heart murmur, and yet I've been able to be courageous, believing in myself. But over time, the murmur deteriorated into a leaky heart valve. Something happened within me that caused me to lose heart. This is what it was: I had to make the decision to believe God, when believing in Him was not enough. The decision to believe in Him can be depressing—especially if you have an ego. The ego tells you to investigate everything and only do what you feel comfortable doing. You can see how that's a problem dealing with God; 98% of the time He instructs you to do something you're not comfortable doing.

And why aren't you comfortable? Isn't it obvious? Because there's a door still open to your past—a leaky heart valve—that beckons you back to the days when your life was your own.

The Desire to Purge, No Power to Produce!

We will leave some things undone in our lifetime. We might as well accept it. In fact, it's our inability to accept this one thing that makes us inferior. Inferior to what? Everything. Everything else realizes that the most important objective is to pass down seed. Not just any old seed—seed good enough to fulfill one more objective than we did.

Today is my fourth day without food. I don't think this is phenomenal. What's phenomenal is that I'm having no symptoms at all, and that my stomach still doesn't feel empty. It's like there is something in there that refuses to come out. In the stillness of the night I felt my heart do something strange. I felt it lift up and adjust itself. This is phenomenal. I'm curious to hear what the cardiologist will say. I know that the Lord is the one who is causing me to go without hunger. I can feel his fingerprint all over this.

Whenever we do something that is completely against our nature, to accomplish something divine, be sure God is behind it, bragging, boasting of His goodness, His generosity toward us. I want to purge. My body desires to purge, but something is preventing her from doing so. This is a problem. When I urinate, I can barely feel my kidneys urging me. I have to be as quiet and as still as a church mouse to hear her needs.

Are we like that toward God? Why do we cry out to the wrong people about the wrong things? Why don't we cry out to the only one who can change things that matter? Like, "Lord, I can't purge! Lord, something is preventing me from walking with you and it's trying to kill me before I can pass down purpose!"

Father, help me to purge, cleanse the innermost parts of me so that I can glorify your name to the generations. In your wrath, Lord, remember your mercy.

Send your abounding grace to restore me to the land of the living. Give me purpose, Lord—a life worth fighting for, productivity that matters to you. Bless me with your covering; protect me from evil. I'm fighting for my life. As I've covered others with my prayers, cover me, Lord. Remember how much

*you love me. Remember how valuable I am to your kingdom,
and remind me of these truths.*

*Cause not my heart to fail. Breathe in her the breath of life; clear
a path in my veins for your Holy Spirit to rush through. Purge
me Lord, for your name's sake, of everything I've done that's
been unprofitable. Amen. Forgive me.*

I Don't Feel Like It

I don't feel like writing today. I thought about simply not doing
it. I deserve a break, right? Who writes non-stop anyway! One day
off isn't tragic, is it?

Then I remembered how many times I didn't do something
because I didn't feel like it. Where did that get me? Since I've been
keeping the Sabbath, and committed to reading the Messianic Jewish Weekly Reading Portion along with reading the bible annually
from cover to cover, I've learned something about myself. Actually
I've learned something about humanity. We rely too much on how
we feel.

Athletes often get depressed when their athletic life comes to
a halt because of one thing: they abandon their routine. When we
only do what we feel like doing, we miss out on a very important
principle—perhaps the most important principle our fathers should
have taught us: How you feel is irrelevant.

I don't say that easily. Trust me. My commitment to a Messianic
way of life took years to establish. But when I finally surrendered
to the routine, yielding to it whether I felt like it or not, a new
character trait emerged in me. I am disciplined.

Discipline says do it because you know it's good. It does not
consider how it will make you feel. Not to say your feelings aren't
considered. That's just it. Your feelings are considered; they are not
the deciding factor.

When I look back over the things that I've done because they became my self-imposed practice, I rarely have regret. What I do regret is the times I didn't do something that I knew I should have done because I didn't feel like doing it. These things are the cellulite pockets of my life—so easy to put on, impossible to take off. I'm glad I changed my mind. When we do what we don't feel like doing, that which God expects us to do, something cool happens. We move. We move forward in strength and in courage.

I had my first juice today. I probably should mention that I'm on a 56-day dry/water/juice combination fast. I guess that means, simply put, I'm on a no food fast. I didn't mention it earlier because I didn't want this to be a book about my fast. Actually, I wanted it to be a book about nothing because nothing has a value. Nothing is everything in the middle; it's the fluff, the minutia that makes life worth living.

Anyway, I had a revelation as I drank. One word came to mind: rewarding. For some reason, the juice (a combination of vegetables and fruit) was the most satisfying thing I've ever tasted. I didn't drink it because I was starving, although last night while I cooked spaghetti for my husband my foot almost slipped. But today, I drank it because I believed it to be a good decision. See how I'm changing my words? I didn't feel like it. I believed it. I believed that I should reward myself and use that reward as a platform from which to spring with the strength to do my next week's work. The juice, if you can believe it, literally gave me hope. Hope that I just might be able to go the distance.

When I received this in my soul, I heard the Lord in my spirit:

> *"Stop waiting for Me to reward you. The rewards are already in place. Move your life around them."*

I guess the first step is to know God's reward system, and the second step is to do work worthy of the deep satisfaction that comes when you reach that reward. I thought I had nothing to write about. I was wrong.

CHAPTER TWO

Whole "*E*" Ness Changes the Strategy

At The Pool Again

*M*emories of my grandma's pool. Sitting in the shade. Just a little bit of sun is left. Not bad for 7:00 p.m. I swim back and forth. Not a young girl anymore to-night. Tonight I'm a mother, a wife, and a grandmother. But I swim as if I'm young again. I dared myself to wear a two-piece bathing suit to the pool and to discard my clothes before the eyes of judg-ment and jump in.

There was a time, so long ago, that I swam without care. Not allowing my body to rule me. Knowing what was good for her, I soaked her in sunlight, salt water, riverbeds and yes, chlorine. Her skin glistened with youth, toned and radiant. It was void of imper-fections, and if there were any, they wouldn't keep me from swim-ming.

Now at 48, just a few weeks shy of my 49th birthday, I decide to hear my body again. This is to brag of her insufficiencies, and to boast of her inadequacies. Wrinkles and dimples and stretch marks, hinting at stories never shared. Telling about the time I broke my father's heart by getting pregnant at 17. Telling about my two mid-term miscarriages. Both miscarried because I willed them to die. A car accident took the life of one, and I spoke death into the other until my body agreed with me. Granting my soul's request to my spirit, my babies were surrendered. Boasting of my daughter's passing, the one who taught me the greatest lesson of all. You can't tango intimately with death and then casually break up with him.

Back and forth I swim, revealing the stretch marks my daughter left me with when she died on June 3, 1991, twenty minutes after she was born. I own this body now, as if I'm 17 again, refusing to live in the sea of the muddy, gritty, past. I own this body again, and it feels good. I do not deserve for it to feel good. Good is reserved for those who've lived above standard, and I am not one of them. Good is reserved for those who've had no affairs, made no left turns: those who didn't make decisions that should not be mentioned. Good is reserved for somebody else, and yet I swim in *that* pool.

In the days when the grille was burning and the heavy smoke filled the air, the laughter of my grandmother made me believe the world was a safe place and life was worth living. I believe that today, as I swim. And I wish I could stay here, in this nest of comfort, like Grandma's house. But the sun is setting and it will be dark soon.

I can take one more swim because I own this body and I know what is good for it.

Pizza

I've been 177 pounds since Friday. I didn't lose anything even though I haven't eaten in five days. Well, with the exception of pizza. Isn't that how life is? One measly little pizza can seriously make you pay. Not a high price, but expensive enough to keep you from going forward. And yet I have to ask myself, in the grand scheme of things, what is my objective? Is it my objective to get closer to God, just to lose 50 pounds? To boast of going without eating? No. This time, God was right. He whispered to me while I was in the shower. *This time will be different.*

My objective is to move forward and not allow one pizza to hold me back. To use it to produce something even better; perhaps to use it to produce a life I wouldn't have had, had I never tasted.

Obviously, to go without pizza would have been better; I'm not discounting that. Then I could add my name to the list of Greats. But the fact remains; I'm not on that list. My life is splattered and splintered with great strokes of *grace*. I cannot boast at all in my own strength. That is not my story. My story is the pizza story. It's the one filled with portabella mushrooms, onions, chunks of turkey in a seasoned meat sauce, and extra cheese.

Yes, spread evenly across homemade dough, it was mouth-watering pizza, probably the best I've ever tasted—and I've had some pizza in my days. But that pizza held me back. It sat in my stomach unapologetically, refusing to move or be moved. And yet the *grace* of God worked it for my good. It's hard to know what's truly right and wrong without the Holy Spirit's interpretation. In truth, we are all wrong. But God gets in the details and sorts every strand. He says, "She shouldn't have had that pizza, but I'm gonna make it work."

I'm Angry With My Body

I'm angry that I have no control over my body. I can't determine whether she lives or dies. I can't help her to heal. I can't train her to be healthy. All I can do is watch, and I'm angry as hell about it.

Because I have a leaky heart valve, fluid is occupying space in my body. I've tried fasting; I've tried drinking only water; I've tried eating the right food. Nothing helps. Every morning the fluid returns. My body loses weight but not fluid. It will not—refuses—to be drained of fluid. And for some reason, this brings me back to my daughter, Jordan, who died 26 years ago.

I had retained an inordinate amount of fluid. So much that my belly expanded beyond its capacity. But I just remembered something. I remembered that I had an idea, at the time, that if I was going to lose my daughter, the least I could do was take care of my body. After all of these years, how funny that I would remember that, so, while all manner of evil was happening to me that I couldn't control, for some divine reason, I was able to look past it and plan for the future. I was able to say to myself, "Grieve now, but plan for later!" And it worked. While I grieved, I whipped my body into shape. Underneath the weight of losing a child, I was able to plan my recovery. Wow. I'm stronger than I thought.

So now I look at this body, struggling to gain oxygen and blood from a heart that is determined to live, even though it lives with a limp, and I see it differently. Perhaps I should be getting in shape for afterwards. I never thought of that. Hadn't I learned something from Jordan? Hadn't I learned that sometimes you have to face the giants? Sometimes there is no getting around it. In preparing to face them, you can plan your victory.

Yes, I'm angry. But maybe I'm not angry with my body. Maybe I'm angry *for* my body. Maybe I feel something I should have felt a long time ago, but I didn't have the time, nor did I grant myself permission. Maybe, just maybe, I feel compassion. I feel sympathy. I love my body. My heart grieves to see her unable to help herself. I'm grieving for my heart. I'm grieving that without a strong heart, a healthy whole heart, my entire body suffers. Yet, she wears it so well. No one would ever know how tired she really is.

I woke up angry. I woke up bitter that no matter what I tried, the ailment was still there. The only solution, seemingly, was to starve her, to beat her into submission. But even then I learned, the best that would ever come of that is leaner muscle. She, herself, would not be healed that way.

Nope. This time, this body can't help herself. For a strong woman, that's a blow to the ego. I don't like being told that I can't help myself. That means that my body is in someone else's hands. Imagine that? Imagine that! I spent my whole life ensuring that my body was never in anyone else's hands...or their care for that matter. Eventually, a thick layer of protection stood between me and anyone who tried to love me—*that* way.

Lord, if it's not time to heal my entire body, would you have compassion on my heart? Without her, I think I would die.

Go and Sin No More

I never learned how to process anger. I know it's best to find a stress outlet like exercising, but what do you do if you can't exercise? What do people do when their options are limited? How do we handle anger when there is no choice for managing or diluting it? What happens when we have to feel it?

I have something in common with my adversary. When I get mad, I cheat. Not cheat in the way of board games, or even on my job. It's ironic that I would have rules about cheating, and still be a cheater, but there are limits to what I will or will not do. Somehow keeping my own version of a conscience, or maybe I'm just not angry enough in every circumstance, I cheat in some capacity if I'm angry. One thing is for certain, when I'm angry and I do cheat, my main goal is to cheat God.

When my daughter died, I cheated. I'd like to say that I cheated on my ex-husband, but that would be only half true. My main objective was to put distance between God and me. I was angry as hell, and I wanted Him to know. It's easy for me to analyze now, some thirty years later, but I recognize that it became a pattern with me.

I just couldn't express my frustration adequately enough. I couldn't control my environment, my life, and my choices. I couldn't control anything, and who else but God could be behind something like that?

That's what people do when they have affairs. Being at the mercy of anger, they lash out because no one wants to live with being angry. Anger suffocates. It oozes through every empty space like the liquid that fills my sick body now, making it retain dead water. Cain was angry. The woman at the well was angry. The woman caught in the middle of adultery—*she* was angry. Of all things, you'd think at the very least you could control your own body. I spent years proving this very point. But what happens if the day comes when you can't even do that? How do you express your anger if you can't even use your own body to do it?

I used my body as a weapon. I beat it through exercise, sex, and discipline, including long bouts of abstinence to prove a point. I abused it through overindulgence when my anger reached its boiling point. Perhaps my heart gave out because of the abuse. Perhaps the murmur, the complaint, was my heart crying out against me. Refusing, unwilling to be cheated anymore, she cried out that she would not be used for purposes unintended. My heart wasn't in it, and her cry reached the ears of God.

Jesus didn't tell the adulteress that she was wrong for being angry. He didn't even tell her that she didn't have a right to be angry. Jesus says to the woman, "Go and sin no more," as if there is a way to be angry and yet not sin. I'm angry that I'm not perfect. I grieve over it daily. If I were perfect I could accomplish so many things. I could be like God—I think. But now that I think of it, maybe being perfect isn't enough to be like God. The bible says that Jesus, who being in very nature God, set it aside. It wasn't flawlessness that got the job done; It was obedience to the Father's instructions.

Jesus set aside his flawlessness to be and do something flawed. He literally stepped into a restricted, imperfect vessel and still managed to do extraordinary things. How can you be in an imperfect situation and still accomplish the task perfectly? This has been my lifetime frustration. Be angry, He said, and handle it perfectly.

I Woke Up This Morning: ME

I ate last night. Badly. I started off convincing myself that I have the right to eat. Then it turned into an angry tantrum. Who ever heard of having to fast in order to dry their body out of fluid, and to pray to God that the heart can heal itself?! And so I ate. I ate dinner and ice cream and chocolate covered peanuts, and finally the pie that I said I'd never touch again.

All of my hard work—wasted. That's the story of my life. I was angry with God and He wasn't angry with me, and that made me angrier. I wasn't even given the dignity of a good fight. I went to sleep angry, and it inflamed my body, as I knew it would. Perhaps I even did it because those were the results I was looking for. I cheated, like always. Nothing has changed. I haven't changed and the knowledge of this put me in the place I needed to be. Being angry with myself, angry with my life, angry with God; but then I did something different. I got out of bed, and I praised Him.

I woke up this morning completely me. Makes me wonder who I was before. It's as if I was in some sort of coma, and suddenly I've awakened from it. Everything looks different from here. I'm seeing through another lens. Peculiar.

How much of your life has been faked? How many days did you sleepwalk through? I came into the wilderness to find her, and here she is. She found me, the disappointed heartbroken one who can't connect to anyone or anything. She's here, and she is who I came looking for. I need to have a conversation with her. It's a conversation that she has needed for a very long time. Had this conversation been a part of her life from the beginning, perhaps her choices would have been different.

Self, me, the me who hides at other times, trying to please and be pleasing until the floodgates break and the pressure builds to explosion and you burst on the scene, making your debut. *That* self—I'm glad I have your attention. What I've got to say to you will probably make you vomit. Take some deep breaths; it's going to be a minute.

Life is not always going to be filled with laughter, second chances, love, and good health. There will be bad times. There will be occasions for heartbreak, disappointment, and drudgery. In fact, there will be seasons when all that is required of you is that you survive. And your delight in such conditions is not even a factor. You've got to accept it. That's real.

No longer can you come and go as you please, weaving in and out looking for hot spots of paradise. The trick to living the magic that your soul desires is commitment: Connect on the ground level. Be committed to the fluff. Committed to the bullsh*t. Because within the bullsh*t, at its very center is the truth, and you can't get to it without getting dirty.

So you've discovered that you won't always be desirable and you won't always have desire. You've discovered that your heart will be in it one moment, and in the next moment, you will lose heart. Learn how to say, "So what!" Shrug your shoulders and say, "Oh well!" Try it. You won't always please everyone, and everyone won't always please you. But that doesn't absolve you from the assignment. Your excitement level doesn't cancel the appointment. There's still sh*t to do.

So go on, cry about it. Grieve good and hard. Grieve that life is not a crystal stair. Grieve that tears don't move God, obedience does. Grieve today, and tell yourself that life is not worth living if you have to do things you don't want to do, in a way that you would rather not do them. Grieve because you want to give in to yourself and give up on life, and you can't. He won't let you. Grieve because you think you've done enough and the rewards haven't been as fulfilling as you assumed they'd be. Grieve because life doesn't give the best orgasms, and death promises release from all burdens. Grieve. Grieve, self, grieve! Have a grieving party and know that grief is part of the journey. Accept the fact that though you grieve—and grieving sucks—there's still sh*t to do tomorrow.

I'm Every Woman

The truth is, I haven't been very good to my heart. Sometimes I fed my body things my heart couldn't handle. I fed her things that tasted good for a moment, but she couldn't handle the after effects. I fed her food she simply couldn't process. It was foreign to her. After the occasion was gone and the smell of sweat no longer lingered in the air, she was left to deal with the memories.

The mind can be a cruel taskmaster, telling the heart to "just get over it." Can you really just get over loving inside and outside of marriage? My heart doesn't think so. Sometimes we become heartbroken and we don't even know it. I think my husband and I married one another in a heartbroken state. Though he denies it, I think we were heartbroken when we brought our pieces together.

Yes, I've been married three times, and have loved my share of men. I am the Samaritan woman. I am the woman at the well—thirsty, but never able to get the need met, or have the thirst quenched. I am the woman caught in the midst of adultery, thrown before the feet of Jesus. That's me. I am Bathsheba, bathing on the rooftop in full view of the king. I am Eve, wandering off to the sound of a strange whisper, toward a tantalizing smell, to savor the sweetness of fruit I had no business eating, neglecting the side of my husband. I'm she.

I'm Jezebel, trying to obtain for my husband what God has kept back from him. I'm Gomer, justifying serving myself because the men of my culture are getting away with murder. It's all me. I'm Rahab, making a deal with Joshua. Smart enough to understand when the tide is changing and it's time to trade in the garments of prostitution, adultery, and harlotry. Don't you see it?

I'm the whore of Babylon, where the blood of the saints can be found between my legs and lingering on my breasts. The tears of heartbroken men were my vindication. The more they wept, the deeper they hurt—never able to fulfill the craving I left in their flesh— for me, sweet vengeance was enough.

I was angry with God, angry with myself, angry with men— until there was no more—until the anger subsided and the daylight broke. Then I met a man who told me all about myself. He spoke honestly to me about the deep things no one else could see, and I stopped being angry. When the anger subsided, I no longer craved their blood, nor their sweat or their tears.

I began to cry for them. I expected them to be stronger. I expected them to be cruel. I expected them to live up to their reputation. Where were the dogs at? When the morning sung, and the dew of the day rested on my window *pain*, I cried like a baby. The dogs were no match for a bitch like me. They were merely mortal, broken-hearted men, disenchanted with their jobs, their lives, their god. And me? I was every woman who promised them with the sadness of my eyes and the softness of my lips what I knew I could not deliver.

They became broken before me and I was disappointed. Devastated, really, by the fact that men bleed. Astonished that they limped from injuries suffered long ago, I discovered that there were no super-heroes. There were no villains. I was every woman; it was all in me. So I made them believe. But it was a lie.

CHAPTER THREE

Whol "*E*" Ness Protects Your Life

Frozen Yogurt Is Not a Snack

*W*hen you start out making excuses for everything, it's hard to stop. I learned this early on, and though I tried to be better, I simply found more ways to justify bad behavior.

I didn't think it was fair that men got away with murder. On the one hand, I loved men. Having been raised for most of my childhood by a single father, I had empathy. But the more empathetic I was towards men, the more I hated myself. If men were so good, then women are so bad. Women are natural complainers. They are never pleased; nothing is ever good enough for them.

Women are clingy, and needy, and bratty, and looking for a father figure or a savior. This is what women bring to the table, regardless of how it is disguised. Women don't truly love men. They need them for their life force. Then, like a praying mantis, she cuts off the head of her husband and disposes of him. 'Cuz a good woman can live without men. Right?

If women loved men, if they truly respected men, men would be loyal, faithful consumers. "So the fault is in the woman," I told myself privately and given the occasion, in public. But taking all of the blame means taking all of the power. If the woman were truly to blame for the plight of the man, then a good woman could redeem him. *Was that true?* I wondered. *Was it at least true enough?*

Unfortunately, that hasn't been my experience. See, Eve was a good woman in the beginning, and Adam was a good man. But in the midst of a good thing, there is room for bad when we turn our backs on God. When we turn our backs on God's instructions, there is no good thing there.

I'm always trying to justify. Justifying the man. Justifying the woman. Justifying myself. When God says, "No snacking between meals," I decide that He doesn't mean what He says. I decide that there is a way around it. He meant chips. He meant between breakfast and lunch. He didn't mean dessert.

Seldom do we come back to God and say, "What did you mean, exactly?" And that's where the snake got Eve. Did God really mean what He said? If I can just get you to doubt the meaning, I can move you out of the realm of understanding. Understanding the meaning of life? No. Understanding that what God said is what He meant. And He's not afraid to take the blame.

It's Not About Me. I'll Try to Remember That.

I'm impressed with my body. She has a hidden strength that I seldom praise. It's neither in her beauty nor in her physique. Those things were given to her, and frankly she's done nothing to preserve them. But in her ability to persevere, I'm impressed with my body's fight. I'm impressed with her determination. She's resilient. She doesn't give up easily. And give in? Rarely!

I remember giving birth to my youngest son. The midwife and the nurse were mesmerized. They proclaimed with amazement that one side of my body was yielding, but the other side was not. They massaged my flesh, contending with her, wrestling with her, negotiating and wearing her down, so that Israel could be born. I never forgot that. I should have warned them that I'm a summer baby—a Gemini, to be exact. Often, I find myself negotiating with my flesh like those midwives. The toughest negotiation is the line between the two sides of the Gemini, because each side thinks it's all about her. When I don't yield to the counsel of the Holy Spirit, my life tells on me, reflecting my zodiac sign.

From my window, I can see Dick Gregory. It's a running joke between my husband and me because he is fascinated that we live in the same building as this profound legend. Every time my husband walks through the parking lot to get to the door, he announces whether or not Dick Gregory is home, based on the presence of his car.

Mr. Gregory is making his way to the door. He walks like an old man now, worn down by the years he's carried on his back, in his shoulders, across his mind, and engulfing his heart. One day I'll be there. I think this while I watch him. I pray that I'll be worthy of that walk. I pray that I will have touched enough lives to earn that walk.

I don't want to walk like an elder just because the years have visited me. I want to walk like I wasn't the only one I cared about in my universe. I want to walk and have the young watch me from their window and wonder about who I was. In order to do that, the division in me cannot be my main focus. At some point, I have to agree with me long enough to get something worthy done in this life.

Nobody Knows, But God

My doctor keeps forgetting what's wrong with me. She keeps telling me that what I'm feeling and what my body is doing is normal. Then I remind her that if she doesn't find what's wrong with me, I can die. And I'm not kidding.

By accident, on a fluke, I saw her physician's assistant and he found the root of my condition. Without him, I would have been told that I was just experiencing the normal process of aging. God made him see me that day. He ordered my steps, appointed my days, and as a result, that physician's assistant saved my life.

How often are we told that there is nothing wrong with us when our bodies are screaming otherwise? We're convinced that we don't know ourselves, or that someone else knows us better—and what choice do we have, but to believe? Who are we? We're not doctors! What right do we have to research and self-diagnose?

I should never have watched *House*. I escaped watching it when it was on regular television, but for some unknown reason, I became obsessed with it years later, watching every episode, in every season—some twice! And when it ended, I felt my heart drop. House was obsessed with getting to the root. Forget the facts, he needed the truth. It drove him nearly insane and made him impossible to live with, but I fell in love with him more and more each night. Secretly, we were so much alike. It's because of House that I took ownership of my own body.

Sounds silly, but it's true. I realized that most doctors, try as they do, are human. Many lack the passion, very few seek the answers, and even fewer believe. Believe in what? Believe in what they believed when they first started. And that's why the physician's assistant saved my life. Many women die of the very malfunction beleaguering my heart. They pay no attention to the whimpering in their souls and the cries of their organs, as their bodies tell them that something is wrong. They just hammer harder, hoping that willpower will drown out the cry for help.

They tell their bodies no help is coming. Do better. Try harder. Be prettier, become smarter. Stop whining, stop nagging, and stop complaining. Be stronger! No help is coming. They won't find what's wrong with you. Nobody knows how to fix your broken heart—they can't even find it—so you will just have to die.

I Cried Today

I cried today. I sat in the tub weeping like a baby. I'm at my daughter's house. No one is home. For some reason, being here, where I'm used to being the caretaker—a stark difference from being at home with my husband, who dotes on me—I'm gravely aware of the danger I'm in. Not only am I aware of it, I'm afraid of it because my children need me. If anything happens to me, they are orphaned. Their father lives in another country. They may never feel his arms around them again, though every year he promises.

I can't say that his being there is entirely his fault. We were 17 when we met. I still remember the way I thought and felt. Thirty-two years later little has changed. I became pregnant two weeks shy of my 18th birthday. I was a virgin with him, and of course got pregnant the very first time. Locked somewhere between innocence and stupidity, I was shocked, even though I had been educated about such things.

Determined to have an abortion and get back on track, I did not go to my parents. My parents weren't religious in the sense of being rigid and unoriginal, but they were religious in the sense that they attended church regularly and tried to love God, keep his commandments, and teach their children to respect authority. My father remarried when I was 12, after being a single father for many years following the separation between him and my mom. Though I never called my stepmother, "Mom," she was included under the umbrella of "my parents." I held only the name back from her, fearing that if I released it to her I might never have a chance of connecting to my birth mother again.

Yes, at 17, I reasoned within myself that although my stepmother was not my mom, she certainly was my parent. To withhold that authority from her would be disingenuous, so I did not confide in her or my father. I concluded that my parents were not the ones to go to when I found myself pregnant. I went to my mom.

Like only a mom can, she sensed it. She took me to breakfast and began to have the *grown folks* talk with me. A talk that was unorthodox, I thought, between a mother and her daughter. Oh how I wished that talk could have happened 16 years earlier. I wished that closeness had been established when I was a toddler. I wished it had cradled me through my preschool and elementary years. I wished that talk had found me even a month earlier. But it hadn't. My eldest son was destined to be born. My mom's talk came too late. I was already pregnant.

I wasn't showing, but I was, in fact, already pregnant when we ordered the lumberjack breakfast. And although I wanted an abortion, God held me responsible for my actions. Yes, even at 17, and I vowed to live with the consequences of my decisions. Choosing to keep my son was largely due to the fact that I grew up motherless. I had a birth mother, and I had a stepmother, but somewhere in the middle I lost something in translation. Lost in the shuffle of the divorce confusion, I found myself to be the daughter of two women, but incapable of truly making either one of them the thing I needed, the one thing I wanted so badly: something normal, something natural, something filled with blood.

So I cried in the tub, in my daughter's house, because I don't want my children to lose me. I'm their parent. I'm their blood—the invisible source that gives meaning to their belly buttons.

I Lost Time

I remember sitting at a desk at the church I grew up in. I was serving at the right hand of my childhood pastor and I had to call a previous boss for something I needed from her—I don't even remember what it was now. Funny, how that is. When she heard my voice she was excited to hear from me. I loved her, in a strange way. I didn't know her personally on any level, but she was the epitome of a strong professional woman.

Although she was a principal at a local elementary school, she could have held any CEO position in corporate America. That's the kind of power she possessed, a certain gravitas that makes both genders marvel. She had always been impressed with me. Seeing in me a young version of herself, she expected great things from me. I failed her as I failed all of my bosses and everyone who ever looked at me. Shaking their heads in disgust. Some said it out loud, some under their breath, some in silence, and some weren't even willing to look me in the eye. "What a waste of life."

They expected greatness of me. I had all of the makings of greatness but I never became great. I chose the road less traveled, the harder road, the one riddled with mistakes, bad choices, hideous decisions and terrible outcomes. Laden with fallbacks, setbacks and "unable to go forwards." Worse than anything else was my own inability to accept either destiny. I wasn't willing to be great because the work that it required was tedious to me. I refused to become a drone, sitting at a desk in a cubicle, taking orders from those who wasted time on things that didn't matter to me.

In my arrogance, I imagined a better way. But even in the better way I did not excel. A man once told me that I was like wasting water, I would not excel. His words still ring in my ear. Dead water. A cesspool. That's how my old boss saw me. I was raw talent, gifts never unpacked, sitting there in the basement of my life like yesterday's photographs. Only good to pull out and show the grandchildren what used to be, back in the good old days.

Water, dead, like the swelling in my body, drowning me daily because the doctors can't explain it. Everything in me is healthy and yet the dead water is weighing me down, immobilizing me.

I served my pastor many times in my career. Sometimes I was paid. He was a great man of God and he deserved the unpaid work he got from me. I gave him my dedication, my loyalty, and my overtime. I sacrificed benefits, accolades, and support because he earned those things from my God. To those on the outside, my talent has been a waste. In fact, at times my life has seemed wasted, even to me. I often wonder if anything I've ever done has mattered. Was it all dead water? Did I lose time? Did I spend my life carelessly?

I got up to write in my calendar and realized that somehow I lost days. I don't remember losing them. I thought I wrote every day, and of course, I did. But apparently I didn't record where I usually see it. I think that's how life is. We figure if we can't see it, it didn't happen. But that's not reality, is it? I lost time on paper, but in real life, a whole lot got done that no one saw.

Days Like These

Yesterday was a hard day filled with old songs, baking, barbecuing chicken, and heartbreak. My sisters and I gathered in the kitchen, being who we've always been—blood-bound. We talked about things you can only share with a sister. Cuts so deep they don't even bleed; betrayal so calculated you wonder if there ever was any love there. Crying and laughing and crying again, we spilled our pain and shared one another's burdens.

The kids are grown and here we are where we said we would be. I noticed that when one is in pain, little else matters. Food loses its flavor, life loses its purpose, and all you can do is concentrate on the hurt. I think we're fascinated by pain. We examine it closely, mesmerized by its grip. How can something so intangible hold so much power? And so we are hypnotized, captivated, clinging to it like a ragdoll—and we are children.

You wonder silently, secretly, if it will ever stop hurting; and then one day, when it does, oddly enough, we never remember the pain, only that it existed once upon a time. Before it taught its course.

Maybe, just maybe, there are circumstances outside of my control. Maybe I didn't cause myself to be sick, and maybe I can't blame myself. Maybe I'll never figure it out. Can I live not knowing all things? Can I believe God—believe that He exists and believe that He is a rewarder of those who diligently seek Him—and have that be enough for me? Can I concentrate on Him and believe that the truth will become plain? Not just plain enough to see, but plain enough to know the next response? Maybe I don't need to be right in order to respond. Maybe I just need to bring back God's report and do nothing about it until He tells me to.

CHAPTER FOUR

Whol "*E*" Ness Reveals the Breach in the Contract

The Cheat

I've been cheated on before, and I've cheated. It's a vicious cycle and it seems it never truly ends...this cheating thing. It makes you staggeringly tired. The exhaustion is really beyond description. "Vengeance is mine," says the Lord, and He's not kidding. No one gets away with anything. One way or the other, you will do the time. And if you cheated God, clear your plate; you're gonna be awhile.

But then, when you least expect it, the correction stops. It's enough. In the same place where God says that we are not His people, we become the people of the Most High. It takes a lot to get to the center. It's arduous, not meant for everyone. The smell is horrific. It's darker than the coldest night. It's dirty, and it's scary. If you have any sense at all, you'll cry like a baby and start crawling home. But you can't go back.

The thing about making your way to the center is that there is no turning around. It's too tight. It's a one-way street. Part of you wants to return to paradise where your eyes were closed, and your mind was blinded. You long to go back to the place where you were oblivious, and the truth didn't matter—back to the place where you had a childlike heart and believed everything and everyone. But the part of you that desires truth is being pulled like a magnet to the center: to the core, through the manure, and no matter how hard it gets, you are pressed to be there. There you know you will see and hear truth refined. Truth too hard for you to handle. Truth that burns. Not everything is good. Not everyone is righteous. There is evil in the world, and it's not always in the cannibal, in the murderer, or in the terrorist.

Sometimes the evil is in your own backyard. It's in your husband's touch, in your wife's words. And part of you prefers the darkness to the light. You prefer the lie, because our own vanity prefers what's false to God's truth. God's truth is too hard to handle. It burns, it maims, it cuts, and it severs. Nothing about that sounds good and yet here we are, stuck between the fantasy and the reality; everything in us desiring to go back, but everything about us is pressed to go forward.

Almost against our will, we come begrudgingly to the light. It hurts; damn, it hurts. But it hurts so good. As John Mellencamp crooned, "Sometimes love don't feel like it should unless it—hurts so good."

Test All Things and Hold On To That Which Is True

It's hard to believe anyone. I mean, to truly believe them. To believe *in* someone is a challenge equally worthy of doubt. Yet, God expects it from us. Not only does He expect our belief, it is impossible to have relationship with Him if belief is absent. It's His core term. Hmmm. That's strange. How can He expect belief as a condition of relationship if some are still evaluating His existence? Well, that's where He challenged me.

See, our version of belief means that we place all of the burden on the other person. I believe you; therefore I don't need to do anything. The work is all in your hands. How nice for us! But that's not what God is saying.

To God, belief is directly tied to works. It means that you intend to prove the person. In other words, there is never a time when you believe someone entirely. Like House says, "Everybody lies." Even if it is a little white lie intended to spare your feelings, it's still a lie. You may take pleasure in believing a lie, but again, the reality is that a lie was told.

In God's case, God is telling us that the work is shared when you believe—or believe in—someone. You invest belief with expectations of delivery. God doesn't expect us to believe in a fairy tale. He expects to be tested, tried, and proven. In fact, he challenges us to do so because God is big on delivery. He says: *Those who come to me must first believe that I exist, and then believe that I am a rewarder of those who diligently seek me.*

So believe, expecting delivery. Here's the thing, though: you can't believe that God will give you whatever you want. Believe what He says, expecting that He will deliver. What will he deliver? What you need. He will deliver the assignment, the work. Your work will meet His work. As diligent as you are, He is equally diligent!

Now, once you've learned that principle, add to it how you treat yourself and others. When you believe someone, give them room to deliver. Don't give them all of your heart, all of your mind, all of your soul, or all of your strength. Give to them proportionally according to what the assignment requires. If you give your child instructions to go to the store, and the money to bring back the product, expect that they will do it. Believe that they will do it.

If you give a subordinate a job expect that they will deliver, believe that they will deliver; give them the tools necessary for them to deliver, and then believe that they will. Expect your spouse to be faithful. Expect for them to be loyal. Give them the tools that they need in order to deliver that expectation. Believe that they will.

But—and here is the big *but*,—if they don't deliver, do your checklist! Did I work my end? Did I believe they could do it? Did I give them room to deliver? If my answer is yes, and they didn't deliver their end, our lack of belief in them regarding *that* assignment is justified. But—and here's an even bigger *but*—be careful, because God always delivers. Where God is concerned, if your results are wrong, the fault lies with you. Use the same barometer to measure the work of others that you use to measure your own.

Sometimes We Just Need Help!

Sometimes I'm wrong, and I can't imagine it. The thing about being wrong is that it makes you doubt yourself on a very rudimentary level. How could I be wrong? I lifted every rock; I've turned every table. I just know I'm right and still, I'm wrong. For some reason I've grown so accustomed to being right that wrong feels foreign to me. It's not my place of comfort, but here's the thing—sometimes, we really are wrong! I mean, really, wrong? Whodda thunk it?

I was so mad at my cardiologist. He refused to see what I saw. All of the evidence was right before his eyes, and yet he decided that my leaky heart valve doesn't require surgery. Now, it's not that I was looking for surgery. I was, however, looking for a solution. What he provided for me was a Band-Aid. He gave me medication to deal with the edema. He must have been able to tell by my expression, how displeased I was. Then what? Was he planning to let my heart keep regurgitating because it wasn't regurgitating that badly?

This morning, however, I saw the situation from another perspective. What if he was right? Not about the leaky heart valve and whether or not it was causing my swelling—which he doesn't believe it is, contrary to every medical textbook known to mankind—no, not about that. What if he was right that I did not need surgery? What if he was more right than I was, even if we were both wrong. My insistence on being right about all things overrides my desire to receive a greater blessing. What if the solution to my edema is *not* to mend my leaky heart valve? What if for *me?* there is a better way?

What if I have all of the tools that I need to contend with this issue? Just in the past twenty years the Lord has revealed to me these power tools: Walking and water are fatal to obesity. Apples, eggs, and cheese are your staple. No snacking between meals. Listen to your body; she talks to you. Fast, purge, reject certain things at certain times; she will tell you what and when.

What if, in my situation, His *grace* is sufficient for me? His *grace* is more efficient than surgery. Because what is in His *grace?* Instructions. His instructions are sufficient for me! In my case, surgery is wrong. Why? Because His *grace* is sufficient for me to accomplish *more* than surgery can do. So what does that mean? It means that I'm wrong. The doctor is right; I'm wrong, and I can't see that because I'm staring at the facts. I just can't accept the truth in the face of the facts.

His truth is "brighter" than my facts. Man, that's hard to accept. But I have to ask myself, which do I really want? I mean, how badly do I need to be right? Do I need it more than I need His *grace?* That's the question.

What if he is protecting me? What if my facts are right, but where they lead me will be wrong, ultimately? How will my rightness benefit me then? I guess the objective is to end right. Who cares if I'm right along the way and wrong in the end? My doctor gave me a diuretic. Its purpose is to help me with the edema. It can't help to close my leaky heart valve. It can't help me to keep the instructions that God gave me, to begin with. What it can do is buy me some time. It can buy me the time that I need to go back and do what I was supposed to do in the first place.

Take All of the Weight Off

Sixteen years ago, I weighed 133 pounds. I remember because it was the year I started drinking only water, the year I started power walking, the year the twin towers were hit, the year I became homeless, the year I spent the whole summer at the pool. It was the year I spent writing, and the year I started redecorating, and the year I was single. It was the year the Lord told me to take more weight off.

I remember complaining to him. How thin do you want me to be? I took a fit, and he responded, "Bad habits are hard to break." He was telling me, without my knowing it, that my weight loss was temporary. My living situation was about to change, and I wouldn't be exercising as diligently as I had been. Still it confounded me. I was carrying extra weight at 133 pounds? Truth is, I was. And no one knew it but God. See, God knows all things considered. He knew about my heart condition and my bad circulation. God's command was based on All Things Considered. Not just what I could see.

I can carry as much weight as I want to. My life is my own. No one can tell me what I can and cannot do. Not even God. Why? Because He created something called "free will" which enables me to make my own decisions. But not without consequence. I could carry as much weight as I wanted to, but I would reap the consequences that came with that. I didn't listen. 133 pounds was skinny enough. I thought He was talking about my figure. He was talking about my heart.

What If I'm Right?

What if I'm right and God is trying to get my attention? What if I'm right relative to my health? What if I'm right relative to my husband? What if none of this is in my imagination? What if none of it ever was? Where does that leave me? I guess it leaves me in the exact same place I'm in when I'm wrong.

Lord, only you know. Here I am in this space, not knowing if I'm right or wrong. Everything in me is telling me that I'm right, but even so Lord, I bow before you. You have the final call, and your word is law. What do you want me to do with the information that I have? He says, "Just believe."

Believe what? Believe you? Believe him—believe the doctor's report? Believe my body? Believe the medicine? Believe my children, my sisters, my parents?

> Believe the truth.
> *If I believe the truth, how do I prove that I believe?*
> Press into it.
> *Press into the truth?*

Not the truth about all of those reports—press into the truth about God, press into your report. What is the truth? The truth is Jesus. Jesus, please advise me so that I can prove the good and perfect will of God. Please block out all other voices in my ear, and cause me to focus on only your voice. This is too important, too serious to dismiss or to simply accept. I can't receive just any report. What is *your* report, Lord?

You can trust yourself when you are in me. That's what he told me.

Okay, so here's what I think. I think the doctor is wrong. But I think he might be right about there being another way. Surgery may not be the right way for me. I have not exhausted all possibilities. I have not gone back and done all that I can do to secure my own health with the assistance of this medication. Maybe the medication by itself will not help me, but maybe, just maybe, if I take what I'm right about and add it to what the doctor is right about, we may have something.

Maybe the medication is meant to help me do what God told me to do until I can do it for myself, without the medication. And maybe, just maybe, this man in my life is meant to do the same. He is not the solution. No man is. He is not the great white hope. He is the medicine to aid me. That's all any human can do. The medicine that is now necessary because I didn't do what I was told to do with all of my strength.

Maybe there are circumstances outside of my control. Maybe I didn't cause myself to be sick, and maybe I can't blame myself. Maybe I'll never figure it out. Can I live not knowing all things? Can I believe God—believe that He exists and believe that He is a rewarder of those who diligently seek Him—and have that be enough for me? Can I concentrate on Him and believe that the truth will become plain? Not just plain enough to see, but plain enough to know the next response?

Maybe I don't need to be right in order to respond. Maybe I just need to bring back the report he required of me and do nothing about it until He tells me to.

Good News

But what do I trust myself to do? I can trust myself to do the right thing. Hmmm… so I won't always be right. Sometimes I'm wrong. I won't always be wrong, sometimes I'm right. And in between, I have to make a decision. With the doctor the epiphany was easy to see. I could use my business sense to make a decision. I believe him enough to give him a chance. I prove him, and I cheer for him. I don't sabotage. I aid him in his aiding me. I want him to be right.

Ultimately, I want him to be right because I want there to be a better way than cutting my heart open. I hope and pray that if I do my part, if I ride off of his solution, maybe we are both right and both wrong, but together we arrive at a solution.

Give it time. I went to him for counsel; the least I can do is try it his way and do my part to help him to be right. If he is wrong, I will take my faith back from him. If he is wrong, I will seek a second opinion. But how will I know that he's wrong if I don't give it time?

The spies went into Canaan. Sure, God was right; the land was flowing with milk and honey. But they saw a better report, a more accurate report—their own. Their report they could believe because they trusted themselves more than they trusted God. And that's okay. But what wasn't okay was that they didn't hold their peace. God didn't ask them for their report. He asked for their obedience. They were to hold their peace and bring back what he asked them for: the report, without opinion.

Ahhh… I get it, Lord! The report is that I don't need surgery. That's the report. The report depressed me because I went ahead of You. I took the report and ran with it, drawing my own conclusions and crafting my own solutions. I thought the report was the end, but instead it was the beginning.

It was a good report, and I got mad about it. I got mad because I couldn't see further than that. The good report didn't answer my questions. The good report left me with no solutions of my own, and that's what the spies saw. Yes it was a good report, but the good report was bad news. It left them with "still not enough." If the report is good and the news is bad, we are forced to depend on God.

"The truth is," the doctor said, "I don't know what it is, but it isn't your heart." And that left me angry. I wanted good news more than a good report. What good is a good report if there is no good news to support it?

But I knew better. Good news can only come from God. No one can bring good news if God did not ordain it. Anyone can bring a good report, but to bring good news is altogether different. A report tells what you found, but the news is ongoing. It tells what was, what is, and what to expect. In a good report anything could change. Reports fluctuate, but good news is seeing from here to eternity with a continuous vision of clear skies.

So I decided to bring back the doctor's report. I decided to believe God, to test Him on this: The doctor said my heart is good.

CHAPTER FIVE

Whol "$\mathcal{E}$" Ness Heals Your Words

No Snacks

*J*he swelling isn't coming from my heart. It's coming from my failure to follow instructions. My heart is good enough to support my body, with the *grace* of God. Imagine that. I have the heart that I need, with the *grace* of God. Without the *grace* of God, everything is insufficient.

They can't isolate the problem to my heart; it's everything. All things are connected, and yet they are not. My primary doctor was right. My condition is not a heart condition; it's a human condition. I'm deteriorating day by day, week by week, year by year, because my condition is fatal. I am human. And although my heart isn't perfect, it is in good enough condition to get the job of living done—well, even—with the *grace* of God.

The *grace* of God covers all of the inefficiencies of my heart, but I must obey his instructions. His instructions protect my heart from carrying more weight than she was meant to carry. I guess it only stands to reason that my heart would reject some of its own blood. It has to leave room for the blood of Jesus.

For me, a condition that is abnormal is very normal. It poses no threat, as long as I do what is expected of me. If I follow the Lord's instructions, my heart works well. My heart works well—with the Lord's instructions. Without His instructions, my heart works like everyone else's—inadequately. There are no shortcuts with God. No filters. No snacks until dinner. With God, we go from instruction to instruction. When one instruction is fulfilled the next is ready to take its place. Even if the instruction is to rest, it's still an instruction. There is no rest, no time out, from relationship with God. There are no snacks until dinner. There is no substitute for us outside of meditating on and then executing the word that God gives us. Why did our parents discourage us from snacking prior to meals? Because they knew that a snack would take away our appetite for what is good. If we accept substitutes too often, over time, we will mistakenly come to believe that eating a real meal isn't necessary. And we, now adults, know what snacking does to the body—it fools you into believing the lie that you're satisfied.

Pain in the Place of Pleasure

I was six years old when I was molested. His molestation would have a long lasting soul imprint on me. In fact, his imprint will be on me for the rest of my life. I don't hate him. I understand that something, some pain in his own existence built up a place of utter ruin in him, giving him no option but to cause pain to *somebody* else. Otherwise it would swallow him whole. I understand. I just happened to be *somebody*.

Yet, I praise God for him. Had he not molested me at such a tender age, there would have been no need for God to grant me an incredible father: a father who rescued me by becoming the man I needed—my true to life hero.

At six years old I went to live with my father, following my molestation, though no one knew. It was my decision to live with my father. I knew, even as a child, that it is best to be under the shadow of someone good. And how does a child know what's good? By experiencing what is bad, of course.

My sort of bad was confusing. My molestation, I think, was

not of the typical brand. I wasn't penetrated vaginally or anally. I wasn't forced to touch, fondle, or put my mouth on his adult body. Instead, in some ways it was far worse. My perpetrator performed oral sex on me, a child—a sleeping child, no less—confusing forever in me the thin line between love and hate, passion and perversion, pain and pleasure. And after he was finished with me, he put me (the sleeping child) back in my bed, like one would return a book to a bookshelf, no longer necessary, but not discarded. Held onto in the event that someone was looking for a good book, it was a pleasurable read, after all, but once a book has been read, its only purpose is to be passed on to somebody else.

And so my own sexuality became bit of a conundrum. How can someone molest you with the touch of pleasure? How can someone force you to do something that doesn't hurt, though it is causing pain? A question for the ages, it's a riddle meant to confuse me and confound my sense of sexual stability. As I aged in childhood and then in the crossroads of my early youth, my identity became muddled. There was a male strength in me that I couldn't deny.

I developed a sharp, no nonsense, knowledgeable strength that I later referred to as "masculinity." And the masculinity pressed against the windows of my soul begging for something I didn't have. It begged for a woman, a female, a scent that I didn't possess, softness that was stolen from me—an innocence I couldn't fabricate. In the curve of the hip and the protrusion of the breast, in the polished nails and firm bodied youth, with its sweet smell of freshly washed hair, I found myself wanting what they had. They were feminine and I…I was masculine.

But my own body betrayed me as I aged, developing in myself the very things I envied in the feminine. The curve of my hip, the swell of my breasts, the touch of my own hair resonated allure; the attention of men confirmed that although I didn't feel feminine, clearly I was. Pain in the place of pleasure left me unable to enjoy fully what it means to be feminine because that part of me was stolen against my will. And though I found my protected place under the shadow of my father, my father's love taught me how to be a stronger *man*. How could he have known that through his training, *she* would be become hidden in him.

Revenge

In my own sexual dysfunction I've always attracted men with dysfunctions. Unless all men have dysfunctions of some sort, in which case I've always attracted all men. I was confusing to them. Clearly feminine to look at— the Lord blessed me with an appearance that could not be denied—I was, and am, very female. But on the inside of me, in my *core*, I often feel like a man.

I have, from my assessment, the logic of a man, the desires of a man, a man's hunger, his complaints, his way of creatively reasoning, his way of understanding; and so I befuddled men because they found in their arms someone they could not grasp. I couldn't be conquered, wouldn't suffer lies, refused to be betrayed, denied defeat, and always, always sought revenge.

Except my revenge wasn't tainted with teardrops splashed on keyed cars. No sugar in the gas tank. No stalking. No begging. No showing up at your house uninvited. My revenge was love.

It's not that I was never that person. It's that once I realized that being that person was weak, I traded in my cards and upgraded my game. I learned somehow, somewhere along the way that men are starving for masculine love. Though they march as tyrants against their victims, what they really seek is unadulterated respect, and affection that was a demonstration of male adulation. Because I had learned at the impressionable age of six that you can kill with kindness, that you can take while giving, that you can murder with your tongue—and I don't mean with words; my teacher had expertly schooled me—I knew how to seek revenge on men by loving them—to death.

Quite strategically, I set out to cause them to fall in love with what they saw in my eyes. They saw what every man wants to see, an image of his best self. So long as in my eyes he could see himself exactly as he wanted to be seen, my soul became the victor without his ever knowing it. It's funny that my soul did this without my knowledge. I'm simply not smart enough to pull off what she was able to do without my consultation. But when the female soul is hell-bent on getting back all that was stolen from her, she marks her victims.

The only condition was that they had to be dogs. So stringent were my requirements, that if he wasn't a dog, but rather obviously jilted, crippled, a castaway, or easily restored by a genuine woman with good intentions, then he was not for me. My men had to be arrogant, angry, and dismissive. They had to be certain their game could not be mastered. The men I marked lived determined to use women: objectifying them, shutting down any sense of spirit within them. They viewed women as second-class citizens. Not all of them claimed this, of course—any who did immediately disqualified themselves as having no game at all. No, they had to be hunters, not possessors. They were in it for the sport, fishing for the enjoyment, not to actually eat. Those were my men. And I won them by entrapment.

I became what they needed, the woman who respected them. Everything was acceptable; everything was negotiable, until acceptable and negotiable wasn't enough. Then I became who they came looking for—the only man who could get the job done. If they were sneaky, I was sneakier. If they were liars, I lied more. If they were deceivers, I was deceiving, but if they wanted truth, yearned for it at all costs, I gave them truth. I gave them truth until it pierced through the liar, the cheater, the deceiver, and the dog. Yes, the truth did set them free. Love means showing all of your cards, even if that means forfeiting the game. But I was holding all spades. They were free.

Reality revealed they weren't dogs at all. They were men. And each of them desired from me the one thing I just couldn't give them: a wife. I had already given her away.

There Aren't Enough Wives

I once preached a sermon entitled *There Aren't Enough Wives* that nearly got me escorted out of the church. And why wouldn't I be? The church was filled with women. In fact, the men were so scarce it looked as though we were living in a time of war. Where were they? Working? In the Service? Overseas? Sick in bed? Watching the game? I don't know. But one thing was clear. They weren't there!

They had given up on "all of that." They had given up on her, the love of his life, his bride, the Church; and eventually, they had given up on God. Their surrender to being seduced away from their purpose didn't happen overnight. It was a slow dribble, a death by an undiagnosed disease. No one saw it coming. We just looked up and Simba was gone off to Never Land. Hakuna Matata.

And the women, they carried on, conducting business as usual, never wondering or questioning why so many men came to the same conclusion: *Something's wrong!* I can't blame the preachers. How could I? Moses was guilty of the same thing. So concerned about the running of the Church, he neglected the basic needs of the people.

They were on the very steps of Moab, ready to cross into the Promised Land. It was a heartbeat away, and the men began to stray, on the down low. Perhaps it never would have been uncovered had not one leader been seen bringing "that filth" into the Church. I truly think the reason that his judgment was so harsh (Phineas sliced the man and his mistress right through the *core*) wasn't because of the act itself.

Later we see that God allowed the very same thing that some were killed for doing. It was because they were leaders, and knowing that there was a need among the people, recognizing that a solution was necessary, they refused to bring the problem to God. Instead, they turned a blind eye as the men dealt with it privately, discreetly, on the down low, so that nobody has to know. But God was watching.

Women aren't having orgasms. Men are feigning satisfaction. And these are God's people. These are home grown church folk, sold out and sanctified by the blood of Jesus Christ. Is everybody okay with this? Is everybody okay with vibrators and swingers' clubs? Is everybody okay with threesomes and orgies and park explorations, and going cruisin'? I'm not talking about worldly people. I'm talking about God's people. God's people are going without getting their basic needs met, and it has become a monumental problem.

As a result, we've lost faith. We've lost hope, and we've lost respect. We've lost these things for God, for one another, and for ourselves. What was the solution to the problem in Moses' day? The same solution it has always been and always will be. The solution is to come clean with God. No matter how dirty, no matter how gritty, no matter how filthy. It is better for God to know than for our adversary to know and use it against us.

> *Lord, I am a man with unclean lips. I come from an unclean people. Have mercy on me. Surely there must be a way out of this madness; surely there must be a solution for my condition. Lord, strengthen me to follow your instructions.*

The leaders should have said that. Instead their loins burned with desire.

Rare Pearl

My mom wore the sweetest perfume. When I told her this, she took it upon herself to send me a bottle every year on my birthday. Amazingly, to me, it always ran out just as a new bottle arrived.

I went through a season when I stopped liking it. I didn't have the heart to tell her that I bought another fragrance. The smell that oozed from my mom's pores was so soothing to me. But on my body I felt like it wasn't the same. They say that each woman causes a perfume to take on her individualized aroma. This effort I made, to walk in my mom's footsteps, in her femininity, was negated by something. I craved another scent, one of my own.

The problem was that I loved the tradition. It made me feel uniquely attached to her, which I so needed in my life.

I went to live with my father when I was six years old; it was a decision that the old soul in me made, when my parents were going through a divorce. While I never regretted that decision, I did regret never getting to know my mom the way my siblings did. Even as I aged, becoming a young wife, and then a mother, I tried hungrily to recreate what I had lost, not growing up in her house. But I couldn't. It was gone forever. I could only build on where we came together in the future. The past had been shipwrecked beneath us, replaced by different histories and different faces.

My mom had a very large colonial house, situated in the heart of a city just outside of Boston. She painted it yellow with a red door, and everyone who was anyone knew who that house belonged to. She was, along with that house, a trademark in the city. Equipped with a large backyard and ample room to accommodate her eight children and their ever increasing offspring, my mom became an anchor, a pillar, a vessel of wisdom, good counsel, and unadulterated, no nonsense opinion. It was said, "If you don't want to know the truth, don't go to mom's house!" She was relentlessly honest.

In my young adult years, I spent much of my life in her presence, determined to repair a prematurely severed umbilical cord. But, as I aged and began to have a footing of my own, I faded into the background, becoming one of the eight of the children who checked in on her.

When I signed up on a dating website, following my second divorce, I used my perfume name as my alias. It was a cool story to tell, that my mom bought my perfume annually. My name was Rare Pearl. I thought about finally telling my mom that I was no longer going to use Rare Pearl and that she could stop ordering it, but I had forgotten by my birthday, and it came on schedule. As I pulled the bottle from the box, I immediately noticed that they changed the shape of the bottle. It no longer looked like my mom's perfume. The roundness was gone. It's dainty shape and color had been replaced with a sexy new shape, tauntingly strong, yet undeniably female.

Suddenly I noticed the name of the perfume across the belly of the bottle. It read, *Rare Pearls*. I smiled. How on time my mom always was. The perfume changed its name with me. I had an epiphany: I am the daughter of a rare pearl, but my story, what I teach, what I've learned belongs to me alone. They are my rare pearls. My mom showed me who I was, and when that was not enough, she showed me what I do. I give. She didn't tell me this. I realized it for myself, and it was good.

Everyone says I look like my mom. Sometimes I catch a glimpse of myself in the mirror, and I see her staring back at me. And at other times, I see another side of myself. I see not her face, but her ageless words, words from her own mother, words that never die. I add them to the other words that I've kept. Now, I drape them across my own daughter's life, and they become not mine anymore.

Bad Behavior

We do whatever we can to protect our children, but sometimes it isn't enough. I never wanted to be a mother. Perhaps the maternal instinct was sucked out of me when I was vulnerable. I never wanted to be a mother, though I always wanted to be a wife. My reason for not wanting to be a mother may seem surprising. I didn't want to be a mother because I knew that being a mother changes you. I don't mean a temporary change. Not the kind of change that stays with you for a few seasons and then can be shaken off with a new haircut and a wardrobe makeover. Motherhood steals from you and gives to someone else something that you, yourself, still need, even while it's being taken away. And I knew this. Being a mother was not casual to me. I knew that it would suck the air out of my universe and transform the architecture of my plans to include furnishings I didn't sign on for. I knew, in fact, that being a mother would make me a better person, and I had no desire to be better. I wanted to be selfish.

Selfish people get noticed. They get their needs met. They take care of themselves. They seldom truly sacrifice, and they always come first. I don't say this as a criticism. I'm envious! I would have been in that clique, but my eldest son interrupted my plans.

My children, the three living, the one who died, and the two who miscarried late in pregnancy, have been the love of my life. I didn't know that having them would tell on me. In raising my children, I became who I was destined to be. Building them caused me to care about something more than I cared about myself.

It could have been different—All of it. I could have made other choices, but my children were the choice I made. I needed, for my salvation, to choose them. I only have one regret in mothering. I wish I had spoiled my oldest son more. Not materialistically. He had everything. But I wish I held him longer and listened more intently. I wish I hadn't cared about his academics as much and wasn't so preoccupied with his success so often. I wish I hadn't been so tired and so busy when I raised him. Sometimes, when I see him now, married and raising his own son, I want to wind back the clock. Did I give him enough of myself? Did I tell him enough that I loved him? Should I have told him more often? My mind is filled with his toys, the birthday parties, the sleepovers; no expense was too much for the firstborn. But in the eyes of my second and third children I see freedom, even the freedom to fail, and I wonder if I gave enough of that to my firstborn.

I dreamed that I had a conversation with my son last night. I woke up thinking what a good talk we had. I hate that he's so far away. California feels like forever from here. He's there living his dream, and I'm here looking at his picture. We cannot protect our children for eternity. It's not our job. And that's what's miserable about mothering. How do we make the feelings go away? Do they ever stop? I was told that once you have children, you never sleep the same again.

My children are the love of my life, and I never wanted them to be. I wanted to be selfish and self-consumed. I wanted to travel the world with a spray can, leave my mark of bad behavior, and tell the common folk to kiss my azz, 'cuz I ain't comin' home no more. But that lot was not appointed to me. I didn't want to love anyone so much that I worry. I didn't want to wait for the other shoe to drop, dreading the day God says my life has been too good and it's time for something unfortunate to happen.

Do you know who I could have been if I didn't have all of these pieces to reconcile? I wanted so bad to be bad. Bad was what I was born to be, but good overshadowed me and told me to live for somebody else. Now, my fragmented pieces demand to be made whole. If not for my children, what of the grandbabies?

What of those who wait for me, unaware that I have the transfusion that their dead cells need. My fragments make sense when they are strung together, each one resting aside the other until the string runs out and the pearls lock. Life has meaning, even when we can't see it coming together.

CHAPTER SIX

Whol "$\mathcal{E}$" Ness Protects Your Judgment

The End From The Beginning

Stop grieving. Receive strength. Conceive joy. When Nehemiah came back to rebuild the wall in Jerusalem, he spent no time talking about all that the people had done to put themselves in their predicament. There were too many pieces, too many complex components. There were no excuses for God's people, God's land, and God's place of worship to be in such ruins, but there were reasons.

The mercy Nehemiah showed, the compassion he extended, acknowledged the reasons. It was only after he put in the work, built up their wall of protection, and reunited them as a people with a promise from God, that they wept. Funny really, that they would cry, weeping so hard that the Lord had to instruct them how to stop. Have you ever been there?

Have you ever cried, wept, grieved 'til there were no tears left—until your body started protesting against you with all manner of sickness and disease? Have you ever mourned so deep that you no longer had a desire to possess or be possessed by anyone or anything? Have you ever been where God's people were?

Nehemiah told them to stop. They grieved because they had let the dysfunction go on so long. They grieved over themselves, their condition, and the plight of their people until God said it was enough.

Can grieving go on too long? Yes, it can. To everything there is a season, and the season was changing for Israel. God had things for them to do.

When I was a little girl, living in my father's house, I learned a great deal about good home training. My father may have many sore spots in his life, times he wishes he had done things different-ly, but above all else, he graduated magna cum laude in the class of parenting me. If I did something wrong in my father's house, depending on the degree of punishment necessary, 99.9% of the time, I was spanked.

My father's spankings were unusual. Much like a great English teacher I had who said, "Tell them what you're going to say, say it, then tell them what you said," my father lived by a similar motto: "Tell them what you're gonna do, do it, then tell them what you did." My father explained every spanking. Spankings were meant, as my stepmother later said, "to break the will, not the spirit."

He spanked to correct, never out of rage. When the spanking was over, it was always followed by a brief timeout for a moment of reflection, and my father would call both of us (my brother and me) down to talk about it. Then he would make us pancakes and ask what we wanted to do for the day.

Failure was not connected to love, and love wasn't contingent on success or perfection. He was balanced and as a result, I was better equipped to understand God.

It's funny too, in my relationship with my father I preferred to be spanked rather than grounded. I could endure physical pain, but to be put on timeout, oh, I'd rather die! My brother was the opposite. But my stepmother complements my father. She discovered early on that spankings only made me accountable instantly, for the moment. But they didn't affect my decision-making process for the long-term. That's when my spankings stopped, and my discipline was adjusted. Oh, how I hated consequences! I still do! There is something within me that earnestly desires to go back and fix things.

With humans, not everything can be fixed. If it breaks into pieces, "Sorry," isn't going to make it better. Neither will super glue. And so you're stuck with the guilt. Even the grief remains because what is done is done and everyone will always remember it that way. But, glory to God! The Lord writes backwards. It was broken in the beginning, but by the end, it's whole.

The yellow roses spring into life from the vase that shattered yesterday. With God, all things are possible. All things! Impossible to accept, astounding to believe; and yet restoration happens every single day. Nehemiah's compassion conveyed the truth. Stop weeping, stop grieving. It's fixed.

The Core

"My *grace* is sufficient for you. For my power is made perfect in weakness." This is what the Lord told the Apostle Paul. Not a very comfortable place to be, unless you understand it.

I believe the Lord is saying that the world is not a perfect place. Humanity is a fallen race, and because of that fact alone there will be trials and tribulations. Some you will overcome, and some will overcome you. When you overcome, the victory is yours. When you don't, the victory is God's. God will always get His glory. I think then, the goal becomes for us to get the glory as often as we possibly can. When we fail—and be sure we will—when those other times come eclipsing any previous victories we celebrate, we will need to be saved.

In those moments we will remember just how great God truly is. Perhaps that's why in the book of Revelation the anointed cast down their golden crowns in His presence. What matter, what weight, what glory is there in our own success stories when we consider the matter, the weight, and the glory of His!

My husband said to me this morning, "Maybe you just got fat."

Sounds horrible, doesn't it? I was furious with him for two seconds. But because he didn't say it with malice, but rather as someone trying to solve a mystery for me, I had to consider his input differently. I had to weigh it. Was there any truth in it? What was he really trying to say? Surely he knew about my leaky heart valve, my waterlogged stomach, and my blood clot history; surely he knew that I exercised regularly!

But when I had a moment, in the quietness of my meditation, I remembered something. I remembered that God's *grace* is contingent upon following His instructions. God never told me that my heart murmur and my leaky heart valve were a problem. In fact, the doctor's report confirmed God's good news. Yes, my heart has to work harder than normal, but what I had failed to accept is that He gave me the instructions for this heart. He told me how to handle it. He was telling me the whole time, but I couldn't hear Him. He was with me. Every step of the way, He was coaching me. When I listened I was healthy, and when I didn't, I struggled.

My heart had to be handled by the Most High God, because He designed it to be handled only by Him. If your heart is in God's care, He is the only one to whom your heart will surrender. It waits for His instructions alone.

And so I thought about what my husband said. Had I allowed my heart to get out of shape? Yes, all of the other complaints were true, even valid, but in the grand scheme of things, was it as simple as that? My heart belongs to Jesus. No other instructions will do for its care. And when I neglect His instructions, my heart suffers. See, it was okay for my heart to complain; the complaint was not the problem. But my heart complained to the wrong people and the wrong things, substituting lovers, chips, ice cream, cookies, and cake, where prayer and petitioning needed to be.

My heart's complaints to men, rather than to God, resulted in an inflammatory issue.

Why did I use these things as substitutes for solutions? I didn't want to bring my murmuring to God. I didn't, in all honesty, believe He could handle it, or that He would handle it my way. So He did what God does best—He pulled over to the side of the road for a teaching moment. He let me drive so that I could see what would happen. And I drove right into a pit.

I dismissed His instructions trying to separate His *grace* from His counsel, not realizing that the *grace* of God *is* His counsel. I drove away from His *grace* and into His judgment. If I wanted to chase after other gods to solve my problems, He would not stand in my way.

His counsel is my *core*. Without His counsel, my own judgment created a hellfire within me—a sh*t storm if you will—that I couldn't put out, and neither could the doctors. There was only one thing left to do, the same thing that is always left to do. I could run home, back to His coverage, and beg for His *grace*. Understanding, this time, like in the beginning, that His *grace* is contingent upon following His instructions. Those instructions are the very core of the existence in which I breathe and make my being.

Hills & Valleys

Each morning at the crack of dawn I pound the pavement of 16th Street in Northwest Washington, DC. I'm not alone. It seems others have discovered what I have about this street—it's perfect for exercising. Cyclists, runners, walkers and casual strollers pass by familiar faces, set in a routine they share with their neighbors. They are determined to get "it" done.

16th Street is situated on hills and valleys. I power walk. When I approach the hills, I lunge forward, stretching my legs in a squatting position. When the road levels out, I work on my speed, accelerating almost as fast as a jogger. And then when the winding sidewalk dips suddenly downhill, I focus on my core. I walk with my shoulders thrown back, my stomach pulled in as tight as I can manage. I press in until it hurts. The objective is not to hold my breath, but to feel my organs being squeezed until they cry out to me. Until they sweat. DC is full of subtle hills and valleys. In that sense it reminds of me of the land of Israel.

I wonder sometimes why life is so complicated. My son's health insurance was canceled because his insurance carrier thought he had moved and switched carriers with me. A mistake. But then his car insurance was canceled and caused his car to be towed. Another mistake, actually mine. I had insured the wrong car. Sometimes I make very bad mistakes and I look back and wonder how that was even possible. But it happens. I think I'm paying attention to detail, when in fact, I'm focusing on something else. This has gotten me in trouble a few times. I wonder how many times it has gotten me in trouble with God.

I guess I need hills and valleys in my life. I need variety. I need to feel, and to think, and to grieve, and to rejoice. I need to have losses and cut losses, and win every once in a while. Otherwise, how will I stretch and strengthen and get there? If everything were flat, I think I would grieve forever.

It's possible to grieve for a very long time without anyone noticing. It's possible to be angry and disappointed without telling a soul. It's possible to never experience joy, even though your work is efficient: to get so much done, and have absolutely none of it mean anything to you.

Some of us don't ask God for anything because we fear the hills and valleys. We don't ask God for what we really want because it's easier to love distantly than up close and personal. What if, at the end of the day, I get attached and then lose the object of my affection? What kind of dirty trick is that? So we become detached trying to outsmart God. We rarely invest in anything, so that nothing can hurt us. We don't experience too many losses because we've already counted them gone.

Sarah was there. The day God showed up on 16th Street and met Abraham out for his morning stroll. God told Abraham that Sarah was about to experience something she had never grasped in her lifetime. Sarah was about to experience joy.

Upon hearing it, she promptly mocked God. She laughed in spite of herself and mumbled, "Shall I receive pleasure in my old age?" In other words, like so many women say in the depths of their souls, where no one can hear them, "I gave up on joy a long time ago. Survival has become enough for me."

What do you do when God wants to interrupt your way of doing things, after you just got used to the way things are done? What do you do when you've become so accustomed to grieving that you actually know how to work with it? And now, the only thing you truly know and certainly understand is threatening to leave you.

Haven't you grieved enough Sarah? Haven't you hidden behind the mask of contentment as long as was possible? Even if you have no right to receive joy, if God commands it into your life, it will come, dragging you into the hills and valleys and away from the smooth path you once knew.

Elisha asked the woman, "What can be done for you?"

She responded, "Nothing."

But when God gave her what He had held back, she would not, could not let it die. The flat road was predictable. The flat road was enough. But the hills and valleys—those make you live.

The Weekly Reading Portion

I started keeping the weekly reading for several reasons. I noticed that every church preached about a different message, calling it *rhema*: a current word from God. But with the exception of revivals or periodic sermon series, no one seemed to be in sync with anyone else. In other words, one minute you could be hearing about King David, and then the next week be in the Book of Revelation. This didn't bother me so much, except I felt like we weren't going anywhere. We were never traveling along any one storyline long enough for it to become a part of my history, enough for it to bring me somewhere. Although this was good in the beginning of my walk with God, I discerned that something was missing long-term.

I wish I could say that I was smart enough to discover this myself, but I wasn't. I simply noticed that my soul wasn't satisfied. I needed something deeper than a wading pool. I needed to return to my Hebraic roots.

I was power walking one Saturday before I became diligent about keeping the Sabbath when I turned a corner into a densely populated Jewish community. There was a small flower shop situated right at the perfect location, in the center of a hot traffic intersection. But the store was closed.

I shook my head. *Those Jews,* I thought, *why would they close business on the busiest day of the week?*

The next day I walked by that same shop and the parking lot was completely full. I took note. They knew something that I did not. They kept their value attached to God's standard, not man's. And that's why they prospered.

See, this is where people make grave errors. The Jews are not a perfect people. They just serve a perfect God. So many folks waste their time staring at the people, waiting for them to fail, and be sure they will, but that proves nothing. Stare at the God of the imperfect people. Then you'll marvel!

The Jews learned that even if they disagreed with each other, arguing over the very text in which they all believed, some truths are absolute. The Jews don't argue over what God says. In that they all agree. They argue over what He means. They argue over interpretation. Now, *that* I can live with.

Orthodox Jews have a system for getting through the Torah annually and combining that weekly reading with confirming excerpts from the writings of the prophets. Then the believing Jews added confirming words from the gospels. It didn't take a genius to see that this was good. So I began not only keeping up with the weekly reading, but also writing and publishing commentaries, as the rabbis do. That expanded into my own systems for setting goals and objectives, keeping monthly themes for life and work, and getting through the entire Bible every year, come what may.

Keeping the weekly reading portion has not exempted me from my humanity, nor does it promise to. In fact, every week you are reading about the imperfect lives of imperfect people who walked with God. I'd love to apologize to you for not being a good minister. I'd love to apologize because I would be a terrible pastor, transparent to the point of discomfort and pain. The congregation would bleed truth—and sometimes just bleed. That's too much color to handle on any given Sunday.

I'd love to apologize, but the truth is then I'd have to apologize for the patriarchs and the apostles. They too were human. They too had to use the bathroom, blow their noses, and yes, occasionally, hopefully not too often, pass gas. Let's face it; humanity is just not that sexy without the makeup. When examined closely the only thing that separates men from beasts is the will to want to be more. I keep the Weekly Reading because I know who I am, and it reminds me of the person I could be, the one I should be.

Today, I Grieve

I'm not going to be who I thought I was. It doesn't really matter how the story ends: the pieces have made the difference. I think there is a time to grieve. Grieving is important, but then, the morning comes, beckoning you to shake it off. Shake it off because today is not today anymore and we've already stayed too long in yesterday.

Truth be told, what we thought we wanted isn't even the same as it was, and how could it be? We've changed. When we changed so did our perspective. Maybe we were meant to shatter—maybe shattering was the purpose. It's quite possible that while we were whole, we weren't anything at all. A blank slate, a sliding glass door, nothing special. But the pieces themselves, that's what made us different from everybody else.

I remember that I didn't look back; I couldn't when I left him in Israel. I didn't look back because I loved him and my courage was needed forward. He was the father of my children, the man I grieved over for most of twenty years. But when tomorrow came, and my soul knew that it would, I didn't look back at my first husband.

I drove my second husband to the bus station. He left the same way he came—mysteriously, an angel and a demon wrapped up in one bible thumping, hearty laughter that rang through the house and let everyone know that all was well. I cooked for him and cleaned for him and loved him despite our mismatch. But when it was time to go, my second husband passed through my life like sudsy dishwater on my hands. We didn't belabor the parting, and I don't even remember the kiss, but I do remember crying. I remember because I cried over pancakes with my sister. She took a picture of me that day. I still have it. There was so much pain in those eyes.

How can someone grieve over a man she was never supposed to love, never allowed to love, just as deeply as a man she shared children with? And I'm not done grieving. I don't know what the rest of the day will bring. I know that my grief for them has ended. I know that. I know that no tears streak my pillowcases and there is no knot in the center of my belly, in the hollow of my soul, like there used to be. It's healed now, but I'm not proud of what I did to be healed.

I'm not proud that I walked out of the Church, left my title and my bible at the door, saluted the saints and left my purpose for some other sucker to carry. I'm not proud that I took my broken pieces and tried to make sense of them with those to whom I should have been a minister. Greedily, I took from them the energy they needed to crawl back to the Creator themselves. I'm not proud that my rare pearls lost their value to me, that they looked to me like the broken pieces I had become.

Sometimes I wonder if the sickness in my body is payback for solving my problem my own way, outside of the Church, away from her grasp of righteousness. I couldn't bear to look at her, much less her look at me, when I knew too much about her. So holy, so pretentious, she shows up on Sundays with her crotch still sticky from the deeds of the midnight. No one else may know, but I know. I know the things she does in the dark, in the booth, in the back, trying to mend her disappointments with God. I know. Her dress is too tight; her hat is too big. She looks so out of place there because everybody is lying so bad.

The tears roll down my cheeks because I miss Him. I ache for Him and the ache is swallowing me whole. Not my first husband, not my second one either. Nor is it the friends I used as tissues, stuffing them into every space that was leaking because of the breaches in my contract with God. I miss Jesus. So does the Church. And so she grieves.

Broken Pieces

There will always be something that requires our attention. Always. A woman felt a shift in her body. There were signs and symptoms, but she dismissed them. You know why? Because there was too much sh*t to do. She died of a heart attack in her forties. I overheard a telephone conversation today. They were making funeral arrangements for her, but there was no money. They had to set up a Go Fund Me page. She was so busy caring about everyone else in her lifetime, deeming herself unimportant. Not only did the Grim Reaper come calling early, she left so much undone, trying to do things that didn't matter.

Broken pieces. That's what we are. Desperate to hold them together with scotch tape. Maybe no one will notice. And these are they, the ones who follow the Lamb wherever He goes. Well, in theory anyway. Truth is, we are seldom obedient and rarely give our glory to the Lord. Give Him His glory? Yes, of course we do when the utility bill gets paid on time and if the preacher is good on Sunday. We jump around; we cry in our pew. We utter in tongues, "Lord I give you the glory." But which glory are we giving Him—His, or ours?

God doesn't need us to give Him what is His. He already has it. He needs us to give Him ours. Rise and shine and give God *your* glory, children of the Lord. Give Him everything that makes you anything. Give Him all that you have—all of your weight, give it to Him and see what He does with it. See how He converts it.

The text tells us that the Lord came to bind up the brokenhearted. That's me. That's the Church. We are the broken hearted. We are still without understanding. Shifting this way and that, trying to get stuff done that won't matter tomorrow, let alone next week. One day the blood will run out of our fingers, and someone else will dress us and decide how we will be remembered, whether we like it or not. They will make us look like someone we weren't, and we will have no control over any of it. None.

I thought I was already broken from my first marriage, but apparently I'm hard to break. If the first marriage didn't shatter me, the second one proved its point. I was only married for six months.

I have a history of overriding God—a bad habit, actually, of hearing His instructions and deciding to go another way. But there will come a time when your father will say when enough is enough and all of the neatly placed china will come crashing down around you and you are the bull in the shop. Though you never saw it coming.

The old you, but you didn't see it. That's me and that's the Church. The only hope is that He factored that into the greater equation and that somehow even your worst failures are working out something good.

I love deep and I love hard, but I don't love often. Even when I'm wrong, even when I don't show it, even when I don't feel it, protecting myself so that it doesn't consume me, I love even when it appears as if I've walked away. I love, even when walking away was what I should have done from the beginning.

My second husband was not my husband and I was not his wife. We were friends. By mistake we threw ourselves into a pool we had no business being in, and tried to become what we were never meant to be. Our pieces, separately broken, we brought to the marriage bed, hoping even praying that the fact that we both loved God would matter, it didn't. God knew what we couldn't possibly. Our pieces didn't match. Our purposes were not linked, and we found ourselves trying to fit two puzzles into one, regardless of what the vision was meant to look like.

Sometimes, you outsmart the Grim Reaper by bringing your pieces to the one who knows how to convert them, just in the nick of time.

CHAPTER SEVEN

Whole "*E*" Ness Protects Your Hearing

Leave Room

I'm a control freak, a real life "know it all." And that's confusing to my other side, considering I'm also a Gemini. I'm free-spirited, lighthearted and often lightheaded. Perplexing, to say the least, sometimes I appear to be nonchalant, only to reveal that all along, the path I've chosen was camouflage for a deliberate strategy.

I don't consider myself a strategist. I love chess, but I don't play well. I start off with a strategy but soon forget the objective. Easily distracted when bored, non-committal if the project goes on too long, I despise tedium. But some projects are designed to wear you down, to expose your lack of muscle in this area of your existence. I think that's what life is. Life judges you based on your commitment to stay in the game, day after day, playing well enough to stay in it, even when you don't want to.

Sometimes staying in the game is unbearable, unlivable, unthinkable, and unfathomable. We want to quit. There's no reason to go on, and yet we do. Why? What is it about the human soul that compels us each day to give it one more try? We keep hoping moment by moment, season by season, year after year, that life will prove itself to us. We don't give up on her, though we want to so badly.

Saul was about to face the Philistines. He was prepared for battle. The people were ready, but the prophet hadn't shown up to make an offering to God. The prophet was late. Saul did what any one of us would have done. He assessed the situation. Seeing that his adversary was advancing and the people were leaving, he moved out of his lane. He took on the roles of the prophet and the priest, and made a sacrifice to God, or so he thought.

No sooner than he had completed the gesture, here comes the prophet Samuel, ready to do the job that Saul had already done. It was Samuel's fault, wasn't it? Samuel was late! No. Not from God's perspective. It was Saul's fault. Saul was still thinking like the King instead of like the Prince.

A king thinks he knows the next move. The Prince knows that he doesn't. A king waits for no one. The Prince waits for his father.

In one act of presumption, Saul uncovered himself and entered demonic warfare with the demon that advised the Philistines. If God hasn't shown up yet, to whom are you making an offering? Saul was being judged on his personal relationship with God. He lacked what Moses had: The good common sense to say, "If You don't show up Lord, I ain't going."

The adversary wants you to get weary. He wants you to show your cards. He wants you to lose hope. Why? So that you'll move out of your lane. He knows that if he can get you to move before the appointed time, he will steal the ball.

My son played high school basketball. From the stands I always coached him. Yes, I am the reason why so many sports now demand that parents remain quiet. My son was a guard. Sometimes, when his opponent was dribbling, my son would become hypnotized by the pounding of the ball and give his opponent too much time to think. When I saw this happening, I would yell out, "Force a decision!"

It is strategic to get your adversary to move before he is ready, before a solution has come. In doing so, he will inevitably move in panic and lose his advantage. The reason I'm not good at chess is because I like to move fast. If my opponent learns this about me, he will often belabor his move. Not only does this frustrate me, but it also causes me to lose focus and forget the strategy I had in the first place. The adversary pressed Saul, leaving him no room to exercise good strategy, and Saul rushed to action instead of patiently waiting for the adversary to show his hand. He was a bad strategist.

The Glory of God

I think we misunderstood. It seems that we understand some things, but in others we don't have the slightest bit of understanding. God's glory is one of them. We are called to glorify God, and we do this by rising every single day, so long as we have air in our lungs, and giving Him the best that we have, even when our best is our worst offering. Sometimes we preach the gospel and save lives. Sometimes we evangelize and sinners turn back to the cross. But most of the time we must glorify Him through our simple acts of kindness, gentleness, self-control, goodness, joy, love, patience, faithfulness, and peace.

Guess what? In order to demonstrate those things, circumstances must arise that press us to produce fruit. *This* is how we glorify God. We become more like Him in every angle of our lives, even unto death. But there are other times when we must leave room for God to reveal His glory. And in those moments we bring to Him, not all that is good, but all that is real. We bring to the altar our works of the flesh: sexual immorality, impurity, sensuality, idolatry, sorcery, enmity, strife, jealousy, fits of anger, rivalries, dissensions, divisions, envy, drunkenness, orgies, and more.

We bring these works to God as an offering of reality. We invite Him into our world to make us what He will. When we come to God prepared to bring Him the facts about us, something miraculous happens: we see His goodness. God reveals His glory to us by showing us what He can do with all of our "sh*t." I'd use a nicer word, but it wouldn't jar you the way that it needs to. See, you can't fathom using that word in the same sentence as the name of God. Yet, we don't seem to understand that we do all of these things in His presence every day—and we don't bat an eye.

I don't use that word to disrespect you. Nor do I use it to offend God. It's to startle you and to startle myself. Before God, everything is real. There's no room for superficiality or pretense. If it is sh*t, call it what it is. Let's face it; everything we do is sh*t—dirty, worthless, rags if God Himself doesn't show up with the solution. His solution spins our worthlessness into pure gold. Without His solution, like Moses said, "I ain't going!"

Sometimes you have to take a stand with God, like Moses did, and say, "If You ain't going, neither am I!" And this is acceptable. You know why? Because in that moment, Moses professes what is real!

> *Father, it is all dung without You. None of it matters; nothing will matter, if Your glory doesn't show up. But if it does show up—though it be sh*t to me, and I can't see the value in it, though it stinks and it's messy and it may very well ruin me, if Your glory shows up, I'll go! Your glory is the solution. It's the solution to every problem that has exceeded human capacity to solve; and it's the solution to every compound that is filled with disease, destruction, imploding and exploding. With Your glory Lord, the unsolvable is untangled. With Your glory Lord, every crisis must bow, every dilemma must confess, that You alone are Lord!*

So, when we come into the sanctuary, we leave at the threshold our fruit of the spirit. We leave it outside of the sanctuary because there is no room for our own glory. The sanctuary is the one place where we are exempt from our obligation to prove our work. It is the one place where we are not on show. We come into the sanctuary to leave room for You to show up. We don't bring all the good that we've done, because even our good is as filthy rags—sh*t—to You. Instead, we stand before You like Joshua the High Priest, unworthy of Your glory, but desperately needing You to show up. And You hide us in the cleft of the rock and allow us to see Your back—all that You've ever done. And we remember, if only while in the sanctuary, that You are God!

A Second Opinion

Every night while I sleep, the liquid becomes less problematic. I feel my body lighten. I get up numerous times during the night because the liquid demands it, and in the middle of the night, whatever time that might be according to my body's clock, my body is at peace.

If only for a moment, liquid stops filling my tissues and I am myself again. I feel my weight change, even though I am sleeping. I feel lighter; my stomach is not full and bloated. It returns to its once flat canvas, and I have hope. *Maybe*, I think, *while I'm sleeping, tonight will be the night that I'm healed, that my malady goes away.*

But after the clock strikes twelve according to my body's timeline, the liquid begins again to find its comfort in every crevice of my body. I've only found one solution, a solution the doctors didn't give me: Don't drink and don't eat. Apparently, if I deny my body its basic need, maybe, without having to contend with digestion, my heart is strong enough to overcome the ailment.

Nonetheless, I'm aware at this point that I'm in trouble. I can't help but wonder how many people have been where I am today, without ever realizing it. How many people were so out of touch with their bodies that they missed the moment it started? The moment they came under attack from the inside.

I don't know whether to consider it a blessing or a curse that I've lived my whole life paying attention, particularly to my stomach. So long as my stomach felt right, I knew that all things could be worked out. My stomach was, after all, the seat of digestion. Everything that was anything had to stop there, show up there or manifest itself before leaving there, and so I've physically felt my stomach regularly ever since childhood. I would lie down on my back with my knees bent and run my hands across, up, and down my stomach. Almost like reading a crystal ball, I would think, *Tell me what's wrong, I will listen.* And I listened faithfully.

Perhaps that's why I knew that first night. When I slipped on the mother-of-the-groom gown and my stomach protruded as if I were five months pregnant, I knew. No one could tell me differently. Some said menopause, some said too many cookies. The doctors said it was nothing. Despite the evidence, despite the possibilities, they gave me prescriptions to treat the symptoms because finding out what was really wrong with me would require time, money, people, and systems. Nobody has much of those things.

I tried to will it away, pray it away, medicate it away, fast it away, to no avail. In my vanity, I simply can't accept the opinion that I'm getting. How can you accept someone's facts when they directly conflict with the truth?

My youngest sister said, "Believe the doctors and then get a second opinion." Funny enough, I've had three opinions from doctors, even four or five. The general consensus is that I'm not dying. Yeah, thanks. Shall we wait until I am? They don't know what's wrong with me, but I'm not dying. Is that the kind of life I should accept?

If God wanted me to accept it, why would He allow me to detect it, to feel it so deeply, to know exactly, what is happening, though I can't prove it? I'm forced underground to seek alternative medicine—the only medicine that has ever helped me. You can't start off supernatural and then try desperately to return to something normal. So my heart cries out, my soul begs, my mind pleads, and with all of my strength I petition the court of The Most High. *Father, Your daughter needs Your solution.*

I Fell On Both Knees

Sounds religious doesn't it? But it wasn't. I didn't fall on my knees intentionally. And I didn't fall on both of them at once. I guess that shows how stubborn I am. I fell on one suddenly in the winter, when there was absolutely no snow on the ground. I was with my youngest son, running to the store. I told him that it would only take a moment, so it was best for him to stay in the car. He agreed, happily.

I walked calmly, fully composed, in sneakers—and hydroplaned right to my knee. No one saw. I was left with a huge, deeply blue bruise on my right knee that took several months to finally fade. But then, like everything else, I got over it. It stopped hurting. I stopped complaining, and one morning I woke up healed.

It seems as soon as we heal from one bruise, another is waiting to take us by surprise, and that's precisely what happened. My grandson was sauntering a bit too close to the sidewalk, testing his ability to outrun my grasp. Each time I called his name he came running back to my side. But the last time, he had gone too far from the yard and he was nearing the sidewalk, nearing the street. I knew that if I called him and he didn't come, it would require a chase.

Now, I've long since given up chasing toddlers—so I thought. But my love for him far exceeds my physical limitations, so into a poor man's sprint I launched. Again, no one saw me, and I came crashing down on my left knee. Remarkably, as if an angel or demon had painted it, the bruise on the left was *identical* to the one on the right, the one that had long disappeared. I was driven to my knees—one knee at a time. One in the cold, wet winter. The other in the scorching summer heat. One time while chasing after a loved one, the other while a loved one waited for me. I suffered the same bruise, on different knees, during different seasons, in the same year.

I keep asking myself, why didn't I bruise both knees at the same time? Why wasn't it one fall? Wouldn't it have been better to get it over with all at once? Why wait for one to heal before hurting the other? What's the point? If I needed to be on my knees, why didn't He just tell me? Why make it so subtle that I almost miss it?

But I didn't. Did I? In fact, when I got the second bruise it emphasized the first, the one that had healed. The second bruise made me realize that the first one was meaningful. Perhaps I would have just called it a fall and never appreciated its significance. I fell on my knees—one season at a time. So severe were the falls that each time I was left with a bruise. I've been on my knees several, numerous, too many to mention, times in my life. But I've never fallen on them. To fall on one's knee is a sign of desperation, a sign of needing something so bad that you drop with tremendous force. A drop so forceful that your body changes color, that's the kind of fall they were.

> *When I fall on my knees, with my face to the rising Son, oh Lord, have mercy on me. Lord, have mercy on me when I don't even know that I need it. Having mercy on me is the only solution. Have mercy Lord, have mercy Lord, I'm begging you. Have mercy on me, and my people.*

When I got up my grandson came back on his own. He never went down that way again. I can't be sure if his two-year-old brain was able to comprehend what had happened. But I do know that he decided that, after seeing his grandmother on her knees, the time for testing was over. Grandma couldn't reach him on her knees; she only had enough energy to get up herself.

Something Changed

Something changed and I'm not too sure what it was. I suddenly came to the realization that facts are not enough to tell the story. In order to truly have understanding, you need the truth.

I often say that I don't lie, I omit. Omission is a strength. It means that you hold back pertinent information so long as it is not asked of you. Skillful omission secures you a place at the card table. If you learn how to hold your poker face, you can get others to give you more than you are giving them. It isn't that you are lying, it's that you trust yourself more than you trust your opponent.

You can even omit in very loving relationships. The only problem with this is that it can get good to you. So good, in fact, that you begin to omit with God.

I go through seasons when I don't omit. I tell God everything and I tell Him freely. Then I go through seasons when I tell God on a "need to know" basis. I tell Him what I think is necessary, but I don't tell Him the truth. I try to be stronger than I am. I try to be braver, smarter, more courageous, until I get gut checked and I'm curled up in the fetal position waiting for Him to find me. But this time, I'm uncurling my body even with its aches and pains. I'm crawling on all fours until I can walk again. Even walking, I'm limping, but I'm looking for Him. I'm looking for God to bring to Him the omissions in my life.

I've been unfaithful to God, forever the unfaithful wife, because I didn't think He could handle what I had to say. I got weary waiting on You, Lord, and in my weariness, I was unfaithful.

How can you be unfaithful to God? I stopped believing Him. The armies were coming, the people were leaving, and I was left losing heart. I stopped thinking that He was the only solution. I learned that He will let the bottom drop out. He will allow the ceiling to fall. Children die prematurely, and parents can't always protect—and we humans are left to our own inadequate solutions.

I learned that God is scary and that His agenda is not solely to make my life all that I want it to be. I learned that God loves many, not just me; and that's a hard pill to swallow. Though I cleave to the knowledge that He is in fact The Most High God (a truth I've been unwilling and unable to forfeit despite my many disappointments) I'm also keenly aware of where that places me in this broader-than-life universe. Sometimes I hold my tongue because I don't understand, and sometimes I hold my tongue because I feel that I have no right to complain. But I've found over time that holding my tongue with God doesn't seem to be a viable solution. Holding my tongue with God causes our intimacy to wane.

So I come looking for You, Lord.

Snot

No matter how hard we try, there will always be snot, because we are human. There will always be those things we'd rather not talk about—private things no one should know about. They are meant to be kept secret, hidden, we think, even from God.

After we dress up these bodies we've been given and make them acceptable images, putting behind closed doors, in the closet of our lives our menstrual cycles, bowel movements, urination and ejaculation—things that ought not to be talked about—we can accept one another. I don't want to know that there is a side of you that is so carnal that little is left of the difference between you and your dog. I don't want to know these things of yours, and you don't want to know mine.

And so she says to me today, "Pick a color," as I walk through the front door and become one of the many who try so desperately to cover ourselves with something better than what we were born with.

"Pedicure?"

"Yes, please."

"Manicure?"

"Yes, that too," I answer.

"Eyebrows?"

"No, thank you," I respond.

"No eyebrows?" She accuses me with her scowl, as though I've committed the gravest of sins.

"No, I just got them done."

She frowns disapprovingly. Did she even look at me? Did she examine my face before asking the obvious? I didn't get them done last month. No, not last week. Not even yesterday. I'm coming from The Threading Place as I sit in her massage chair. You mean after all of the pain I went through, allowing another person to pluck the hairs from my brows with nothing more than a piece of thread, they're not boasting of my beauty?

Truth is, she doesn't care—no, not really. She doesn't care that I haven't been sleeping, that the swelling in my legs that makes her and her colleagues smirk is caused by a heart condition that is not severe enough for surgery, but too severe to ignore. She doesn't care that my once slim waist and flat stomach are waterlogged and that my medication can't get to my legs; no one seems to know or be concerned about any of it.

Thinking that I am seeking solutions to my fading glory days, they misjudge me. Don't they know that I'm the one who had beautiful teeth, a twinkle in my eye, and a body that made young men tremble and old men blush? All vanity, of course, but they misjudge me. I'm not holding on to my covering. I'm not denying the beast in me. Instead, I'm fighting for my every breath, too tired to stop at the store. Too weak to do laundry.

"No," I repeat. "I just had them done."

I'm sorry that my entire painstaking beauty regimen doesn't suffice. I'm sorry that I use the bathroom like everyone else. I'm sorry that the thought of that makes me less desirable, less sexy, less wanted. Should I lie? Should I dance a jig, sing you a song? Shall I entertain you to make you forget that I have needs of my own?

I'm not just your plaything. I'm not a doll to be dressed and undressed at your fancy, at your whim. Not only am I a beast, but at the heart of that disgusting beast there hides a fragile woman.

CHAPTER EIGHT

Whol "$\mathcal{E}$" Ness Protects Your Will

Fortune Cookies

Sometimes it's so hard to know exactly what God expects from us. We ache to know His will because we don't want to waste time. No one wants to get to the end of this thing and look back grief stricken because everything we ever did was nothing. Even the "nothing" that we do, we pray that God will make it worth something.

The Scripture says that the widow put into the offering tray all that she had. Jesus points out to His disciples that she put in more than all of the wealthy people, because she gave out of her lack. That bugs me. But I'm not sure why. It bugs me that the woman didn't have much. It bugs me that she was expected to give away even what little she had, and it bugs me that she walks away still lacking, still needing, still poor.

It bugs me and it should bug me, if I don't know the Scripture well, and if I don't know Jesus. The woman wasn't giving to man, she was giving to God; and in giving to Him, she gave all that she had, in fact the text said she gave her life's earnings. Was it her pension? Her Social Security? Was it her SNAP card—y'all think I don't know about food stamps? What did she give that was the equivalent of everything she was worth? And why did she give it? Maybe she was desperate; maybe there was no point in going on anymore, so she gave the little bit she had left. Unless she knew that Jesus was watching.

Have you ever given your entire life's worth to the Father because you knew that Jesus was watching? It wasn't enough to give to God in private; instead you needed to make a spectacle of yourself because you knew that Jesus was watching. With the Lord observing her, she stepped to the treasury and gave it all away. Maybe she was saying to the Lord, "I'm all in."

There have been times in my life when I was running on empty. There was nothing left to give. I mean nothing at all, and yet I pulled from deep within me and put in just a little bit more. If you're empty, where does your worth come from? If you've got absolutely nothing left to give, what can you give?

The woman put in nothing. I can hear it now in my spirit. "Father, I have absolutely nothing left to give. It's all gone, not even a talent is left. But I can't leave this place without putting in something, while Jesus is watching. I want Jesus to know that I will even put in nothing to show how much I'm in it."

And Jesus saw, took note, and taught His disciples. Even when you are down to nothing, you've got to put in something. I guess the truth is, we are never down to nothing. Ever. There's always something left to give, even if it's air. Even if it's blood. We have something to give until our hearts stop beating and we surrender our spirits—even then we give up the ghost. Giving exists as long as we do.

> *Out of my nothing Lord, may I give something valuable to You. May You consider what I give to be an acceptable offering. May I give while You are watching, and may I give exactly what You need.*

The woman gave the lesson to the apostles. She gave her testimony to Jesus, and He converted it into a principle that He could use.

I have a tray of fortune cookies on my desk. I keep them for no reason. I crush the cookie with my palm and dispose of it, but I always keep the fortune. Is it because I believe in it and that I rest my hopes on its prophecy? Or is it because I know that even nothing has a value?

Dig For It

I'm sad, and I'm frustrated, and I'm spoiled. Sometimes you just have to do it anyway. There will be great days and there will be good days. But there will also be bad days and "just get through it" days. This is the real life of the believer.

There will be times of ecstasy and there will be times of deep sorrow. We are not exempt from the pitfalls of life. I think the greatest disillusionment believers face is the notion that once they walk with God the bliss will come. It won't. Not all of the time. In fact, I dare to tell you that walking with God can be extremely lonely, very confusing, and earnestly rattling. When the ceiling lifts and money is readily available, when promotion comes, you worry about whether you will drift from Him because of your success. And when the bottom drops out and the adversary is steadily accusing you for what you didn't, or in fact did do, you will worry about your own life!

But that isn't the worst of it. The worst of it is knowing that there is more outside of this simulation; the taste of heaven is like salt in the air when you draw close to the ocean. Walking with God can literally cause you to detach and become disinterested in the things of this world to the point where death seems better than living, and to live becomes a burden.

Which dining room set? Which coffee table? What color do you want the couch to be? Does it match the rug? We're not replacing the rug.

These and similar conversations must take place, and yet you can feel yourself detaching from them. It's monotonous. It's mundane.

The day-to-day life is a grind and so you grind away like a drone; finding escape in reality shows, sitcoms and miniseries. And the balancing act seems unfairly compromised because when you do give to the church, it feels like they take too much.

Serving the body leaves you feeling depleted and utterly exhausted—and for what—for them to barely remember you, or what you stood for? To start off so strong and so zealous, but then to die holding on to your faith as the last grain of sand is infuriating.

The Jews say that when a potential convert comes to them they push them away with one hand and pull them close with the other. "You don't want to serve the Most High God," they begin. "It's a thankless job, serving an ungrateful, unappreciative people who will turn their backs on you as soon as their feet hit the floor in the morning. You'll be persecuted, downtrodden, mocked, confused, and bewildered. You'll settle for less than what you could have had, if you had only stayed on your own…"

"But then," they say, "serving the Most High God has perks that are out of this world. You have the ear of the Creator of the universe. You will never be alone again. You will change lives without even knowing it, save lives without forsaking your own, and fulfill your very purpose every day that you breathe air for the rest of your life."

So the gospel isn't as simple as going up to the altar and accepting Jesus Christ as your Lord and Savior. That's the beginning. That's the introduction. It's filled with paradigm shifts, oxymorons, and irony. It's the rollercoaster ride of all time with a guaranteed ending. But it hurts. I knew a preacher who was well regarded. He had been married to the same woman his whole life and had one son. In the end, he died sick, divorced, and needed a "Go-Fund-Me" to cover the cost of his funeral arrangements. His situation is more common than we'd like to think. I don't know the details of his life's work, but I do know that God is just. Living with that knowledge doesn't make it any easier.

Driving on Empty

So how can I encourage you when I have so little left for myself? How can I tell you how good it is to serve God, when not serving Him tempts me most of my days? Truth is, I can't. I can't encourage you to serve God. Serving Him must be a decision that you are compelled to make.

The disciples saw Jesus flogged, pierced, and crucified. It should have been enough to turn them away. *Is this really the kind of life you want, Peter? Why would you chase death when entertainment is an option?*

Obviously there was something about the Lord that drew them. And in this, I am qualified to give my testimony. Once you spend a single afternoon in the Lord's presence, you hunger for Him like a jilted lover. No alcohol, no drugs, no sex, and no money can satisfy you more than coming close to the anointing.

In fact, it's depressing to live without it. You can't return to the world after hanging out with Jesus. So how do you do it? What drives you even when you've got nothing left? The same thing that drove the Lord: the will to finish well.

I was sitting in a laundromat reading my Bible, underlining and highlighting the text. A dark man in overalls and a backpack passed by me. I only glanced up at him to move my feet. As soon as he passed my seat, he turned back.

"God doesn't like when you write in His Word like that," he said.

In all honesty, I thought the man was attempting to flirt, and I had neither the time, the energy, nor the interest. I had just turned 30 years old. My walk with God was intense. I spent each waking hour at His feet, listening for His voice, stretching to understand His ways. It had been a difficult year. I had returned to the Lord (as I would continue to do throughout my lifetime) after confessing to husband #1 that I had been unfaithful.

It didn't go as I had hoped. I had hoped he would leave quietly. He didn't. We spent the next ten years trying to escape the entanglement we created; dismantling our roots one thread at a time until there was nothing left to do but leave.

The man turned back. He peered down at me, and I wondered if this was my opportunity to evangelize. Perhaps I was being used to save a soul. Annoyed at first because of the interruption, I smiled and closed my bible. Every word I was about to say came to a screeching halt when he took over the conversation as if he were the one in control. He began to talk to me about God, but his speech was unusual.

I'd never heard anyone talk like that before. He spoke as if he knew God personally, as if, he saw Him face to face every day. He recounted the stories in the bible as if he had been there and spoke of heaven like it was the next town over. Suddenly it occurred to me that he wasn't from around here. His speech, his clothes—he didn't even have any laundry! This man wasn't human.

I went to the sink to wash my hands. I needed a minute away from him so that I could pray. *Wasn't anyone else listening to him— could no one else see what I saw?*

He followed me, rambling on about a story he was telling me. He had gone to the mall, he said, and he asked a woman for a cup of water.

I was only half listening because I was praying in my head. As soon as he told me he had gone to the mall, I said to God in my prayer, *If this man is from you, Lord, let him say, 'If you knew who you were talking to, you would have asked for the living water.'*

I dried my hands and turned to face him.

"I asked a woman for a cup of water," he said. "When she gave it to me, I said, if you knew who you were talking to, you would have asked for the living water."

His words still echo in my head, to this day. He winked at me.

Startled, I believed that I had been visited. I wanted to cleave to him, but he was leaving. I begged him to tell me more, but he turned and said, "The next time you see me, you'll recognize me."

That was one of the worst years of my life, and yet, the Angel of the Lord visited me. To Him, tragedy was not something that couldn't be overcome, and Divinity visiting humanity is a normal thing that happens—even on empty.

Holy

It's normal to be mad, or to get mad, with God. Heck, I've been mad at Him the majority of my walk with Him. You can get angry, but don't sin in your anger. That's where we make our gravest mistakes.

Seriously, how could Jonah not be angry? The assignment God sent him on was putrid. Jonah was being sent to an enemy nation to warn them about God's coming wrath, and in warning them, he would give them a chance to repent and be saved. Why would anyone want his enemy to be saved? And even if I could tolerate his salvation, do I have to be the one to deliver the message...really?

Jonah hated Nineveh so much that it nearly destroyed his own salvation. He couldn't forgive the Ninevites for the brutality they had inflicted on his people. Bringing them the message of salvation was a kick in the stomach, and yet this was the Lord's will.

In his anger, Jonah turned away from the will of the Most High God. Is it possible to turn away from God's will? Of course it is, but there will be consequences. See, in order to truly turn away from the will of God, you must first know what it is. Then you can decide to reject it, but when we reject the will of God, we open a door for demonic activity. In other words, you are completely off course, going in a direction that God did not approve of, and that causes astronomical ripple effects.

Yet, even believers walk away from the will of God, only to find out that choosing to walk away from God and into a place of demonic warfare is nothing to toy with. Jonah pleaded from the belly of the whale. From the pit of hell, he cried out, "Lord deliver me, and I will do what You said for me to do!"

What separates those who walk with God from those who don't is that even in that rebellious place, God is working everything out for the believer's good. Jonah learned something about God while he was in the belly of the whale. He learned that when God calls you, you come; and when God sends you, you go. There is no compromise for those whom God has set apart.

Did you notice? By the end of Jonah's story, he is still mad. And that's okay. The Scripture tells us about two sons. One said that he would gladly go to work in his father's vineyard, but he did not. The other son said that he would not go, but went. Jesus asks, "Which son pleased the father?"

Even angry, we are commissioned to finish what God sends us to do. This is a revelation to me. My brain tells me that when I'm angry, I have the right to quit. But nowhere does God condone that behavior. In fact, God made Jonah finish the assignment, even before He explained why the assignment was necessary.

When God tells us to do something, excuses are not an option—not even if we are angry.

Cain was so angry with his brother that he lost sight of the Lord's instruction. His anger spiraled out of control. He could not contain it. When he chose to bypass the Lord's rebuke and to give in to what he felt, he opened up a new path with choices that were over his head.

Murder was introduced into the world because Cain's anger opened up that demonic threshold. Murder was an option that no one had ever considered—until Cain made it a choice.

I am angry with God some days, most days. I'm angry because

I'm sad. I'm brokenhearted. I have an ache in my soul that refuses to be repaired. But I now understand that even while I'm angry, I must finish. I must finish the work of living and everything that doing so entails. The children of this world get angry with their fathers and turn away, refusing to do what he tells them to do. But the children of the Most High God go into the vineyard, yes, even angry, because they are holy.

Forgive Me Father, For I Have Sinned

We learn an important principle from Jonah, such an important principle that Jesus Himself references it. Jesus said that He would spend three days and three nights in the belly of the whale, just like Jonah did. He gave us a sneak preview of something we would never understand unless He explained it to us. Jesus takes on the responsibility of Adam. He takes all of the sins and offenses of mankind and He brings them to the crossroad. He brings them to the altar, to the conversation that He must have with the Father.

He takes the burden, and the dilemma, and He puts them on His shoulders and He goes before the Father. He begs for the forgiveness of those who've done this to Him. Catch this—*He begs the Father to forgive the ones who put Him in this position.* He recognizes their fault. He recognizes what their guilt has done, and He pleads God's mercy upon them. Jesus is hanging on the cross because those He came to save rejected Him. He is hanging there because those He came to heal did not appreciate Him. He is hanging there because he has been robbed, mocked, tried, slandered, beaten, pierced, and crucified by those He came to redeem.

From that position, on the threshold of Hell, He asks that they be forgiven. But, look, Jonah does not forgive Nineveh while he is in the belly of the whale. He does not excuse Nineveh's actions while he is sitting in great darkness. What does he do? He becomes reconciled. Jonah accepts who he is, who he reports to, and what his duty is, as it relates to God.

It is only then that Jonah realizes why he is there. He must ask for forgiveness, too. He must be forgiven for rebelling against the Lord's command. So while in the belly of the grave, Jonah repents. Jesus is there with him. Jesus is there for Jonah. Just As King David said, "If I make my bed in Hell, Thou art there."

Jesus is there for Jonah and for all of the others who lacked understanding. Jesus is the reason that the whale spit Jonah up, and why the graves were opened when He died to obtain the forgiveness of God for the rebellion of the Elect. It is a *grace* among graces.

"Forgive them," Jesus said, "for they know not what they do." It's almost as though He's giving us the words to say to those who have offended us.

> *Father, they don't know that demonic activity exists outside of Your will. They don't know that even while angry they are commissioned to serve You.*
> *Forgive them for putting me in this situation, where I must make a choice that could create havoc. Forgive them for putting me in this place and forgive me for not trusting You. Forgive me for feeling like you've forsaken me. Forgive me, Father, for I have sinned. Have mercy on me because I didn't understand.*

What didn't I understand? I've failed people along the way. I've been a stumbling block. I've caused offenses. I've caused confusion. I've opened demonic windows that ought not to have been opened, and others have done the same to me. My life is riddled with chaos, not because it was God's will, but because of my own offenses and those of others. I did not always do what I was commissioned to do. I said I was going and never made it there. I got angry along the way and plotted my own revenge.

Oh, what a tangled web we weave when first we practice to

deceive. I wouldn't recognize God's will if it bit me in the face because I was busy sorting through all of the choices and options that never should have been. It was a one-way street, yet I was enticed to believe there was another way. I enticed others myself, not realizing the depth of my folly.

Despite all he'd been through, Jonah did not arrive at the full conclusion on his own. He had to wait for God to send him again. In his anger he fled. In his wisdom, he waited—for what? For God to say that the assignment was still on. That meant he was forgiven, and he was capable of forgiving.

Skinny

I'm sorry there is no other way. I wish I could tell you something different, but I can't. The way to the Father is skinny, and Jesus blocks the throne. I don't know what you call Him. Some call Him Immanuel. Some call Him Yeshua. I call Him Jesus because in my culture that's the name we know Him by.

Even in my mumbling, incoherent, backwards, arrogant culture that mispronounces the Holy Name, I still recognize Who He is. He is the One Who saved, the One Who saves, and the One Who will save again. I call Him the Savior.

You know His name. If you really believe, if you truly listen, you will find Him: for no one has come to the Father without going through the Son, and no one has ever heard the Father's voice at any time, save the Son. The Father draws His anointed to the Son, and the Son pulls the chosen to the Father.

It's a skinny path, though I wish it were fatter. I wish there were another way around it, but there isn't. This is the one time in your life where you simply won't find an alternate route; the only shortcut is the one that's been presented to you.

Jesus is the long way and the shortcut. He holds the righteous accountable and redeems the wicked into accountability. Now, do

I know what skinny looks like? No, I don't. What's skinny in one culture is not skinny in another. And, too skinny is no longer skinny—it's anorexic. I can't tell you what your life is supposed to look like. I can tell you what your life is supposed to produce, but can I tell you which experiences you need to have in order to do it? No, plainly put, I can't.

David committed adultery, and yet after the consequence was paid, God favored the son produced from the adulterous marriage. Go figure. I can't set the standard for your life, but I will tell you the one standard that has been set corporately. I can tell you that we all need a Savior. I am not it. If you examine my life, I will fail you.

I can, however, direct you to the One who will not fail. It doesn't behoove us to lower God's standards so that we can have mercy on whom we will have mercy. All we can do is hold up God's standard to the light and confess that we all have missed the mark. The best we can do is to seek God's face with everything that is within us, even when we're angry. Are all sins and offenses the same? No, they are not, but I am not the one to decide which sins have greater consequences, or what those consequences should be.

The prophet Nathan carefully approached David once he became king.

"There was a man," he said, "who was a traveler coming through town. Another man of wealth treated the traveler to a feast, but he took from a poor man's table to do it. The poor man had one lamb that he held dear, like family. But that was of no importance to the wealthy man. Without remorse, he served the lamb to the traveler. What should be done to this man?" Nathan asked.

When King David heard the story, he was enraged. How easy it was for him to see the injustice. He clearly understood what the punishment should be for an evil man who could take something precious from another and dispose of it as if it were nothing. It was ruthless and cowardly. David declared without bias, "That man should die!"

Then Nathan dropped the gauntlet. "That man is you."

How often we measure the fat on others: we point out what they should do to get rid of the excess in their life, only to find that we are fat in areas no man can see.

David truly was righteous because when he was confronted about his sin, he owned it. The greater sin was not the adultery, but the hypocrisy. How easy it was for him to see the wickedness in the parable. It's like standing before the mirror without noticing the extra baggage that has been accumulating. That can be forgiven—maybe. But when your clothes don't fit and the scale tells the story, well… it's disingenuous to keep saying you didn't notice pounds of your own weight creeping up on you; yet you can instantly spot an extra ounce of fat on someone else.

CHAPTER NINE

Whol "*E*" Ness Protects Your Hearing

Secret Things

J was jealous of Jay Z—jealous that he gave himself permission to lay it all on the tracks. There is a way to be honest without throwing everyone under the bus, and that's to lay there yo'self!

There are some hurts that run so deep they don't even hurt anymore. I don't even need to tell you what they are in order for you to know that I've experienced them. We are a hurt people—a people who've been abandoned, betrayed, raped, murdered, separated, divided, and pitted against one another. We are wanderers, beggars, bruisers and the bruised. Few of us will ever make it back to where we are supposed to be because most of us don't know where that is. Secret things too harmful to discuss have maimed us, things too hidden to dig up, too undignified to publish.

We can give some of us, but not all of us. We can give our poetry and call it rap, because to call ourselves writers intimidates. We can rap about sex, gangs, and drugs, but we can't handle the truth about sex trafficking, genocide, and racial conspiracy. We stay in a box most of the time. We buy houses and cars and things that will perish before the end of one life; but the thought of purchasing bigger networks that can be passed down generationally makes people nervous. We are a nation riddled with secret things.

There was a woman who attended my childhood church. She grew in the Lord and became a well-known prayer warrior. One day, she died quite suddenly. The church was devastated. What few knew was that she was badly abused by her husband.

In my confusion over her death, I went to the Lord and asked Him earnestly, "Why did she have to die?" He told me. *She was tired.* Later, when I heard what her son said at her funeral, I was amazed. Her son uttered the same words that God had whispered to me: *She was tired.* How come the church didn't know until it was too late? Because this was her secret—the prayer warrior was tired of living, and nobody knew it but God.

How does one become tired of living, without anyone noticing? Well, I can't speak for the prayer warrior. I can only testify of my own experiences. We have a bad habit of preparing for death so much that we forget to live. It's not that preparing to die is so bad. In fact, doing so is not just admirable, it's smart. Scripture says, "Seek ye first the kingdom of God and His righteousness," but we don't read the latter part, "and the rest shall be given to you."

It reminds me of the Holocaust. So many people died, having survived so much, right before salvation came. They died because they got tired. This makes me weep and it makes me angry.

Lord, why make your children so tired that they no longer desire to live! What good can come from that?!

I think we get tired of waiting for God. We are a people who have waited for God our whole lives. But, what if God was always already there? I think maybe we would realize that we've been waiting for the wrong thing. We are waiting for God to come— with what? The end? If we are waiting for God to come with the end, then our waiting really is in vain, because He isn't coming until all things are fulfilled. In other words, He isn't coming with the end until it is the end.

We've gotten tired of living, so we are waiting for the end. That's not what we are supposed to be doing. As hard as it is to accept, and as difficult as it is to understand, THIS is the assignment. We are commissioned, anointed and appointed to *live*. We are commanded to give a damn about this place.

Do you know what ants will do if you destroy their entire farm? They will assess the damage, calculate survivors, appoint a leader, and build again. In theory they should give up and just wait to be destroyed. But they understand that rebuilding gives them purpose, so that even if they are destroyed again, their existence mattered while it existed. To not matter is worse than being destroyed.

Sometimes I secretly think that none of this matters. In my arrogance, I stand face to face with God and say, "I will not build again." I don't want to invest anymore. I'm too tired to be attached to anything. Nothing in this life has value to me. Been there, done that. Why should I do it again?

The answer frustrates me because that's life, and I say, *Then there must be more to life than living.*

Sewage Smell

I started to wonder if I've said too much. Unlike my creative juices that flow when I'm writing fiction, I have to pull back and question whether exposing myself to you is beneficial. Will there be backlash? Will my transparency be too difficult to digest? Is it more than one mind, heart and soul can handle? But then I hear in my spirit, *"Write like it matters."*

See, I'm not actually writing this for you. I'm writing it for me. If it heals you, that's all the better, but if no one else ever reads this book, it has still done its job in me. How can I tell you what you need to know based on what I've learned, then leave it in your hands hoping that somehow, some way, it will draw you close to God?

It becomes obvious to me when I think of it this way: What

words would I want to hear, myself? What words would I want to leave my children? What would I write if I knew for a fact that I wouldn't beat this thing, that despite my best efforts—maybe not today or next week or tomorrow, but someday when I least expect it—my time will come and the internal alarm will go off deep inside of me. The trumpet call that beckons me home will sound, and my heart will give in. What words would I want my children to know above all other words? That's what I'm leaving behind for you.

When I was young, around 10 or 11, I read a book from my father's expansive collection. I crept into his library one day, surprised by the many titles because I had never seen my father read. It was there in the tri-level contemporary house on the lake, situated between two bodies of water overlooking the deep for miles to come, that I took my father's book off of the shelf.

A Letter To My Unborn Child. I still remember the title. It captivated me. It was an autobiography penned by a man who found out he had cancer and wouldn't live to see his first child come to the light of life.

With tear filled eyes, my soul held onto each word as if, I myself was losing a parent. The author exposed himself honestly, that his child might know him. The Bible says that we are to teach our children along the way. It also says that the Lord chose—hand-picked—Abraham for one reason: Abraham would teach his children to fear God and to keep His commandments. Abraham was chosen because of the kind of father he would be. He would be a father whose words would matter to his children.

And so in that vein, uncertain of life's guarantees, I leave this work behind, that my children might know me, and know God, and know my walk with God. I want them to understand that to live is to walk with God. There is no other way.

Don't exclude Him in your seasons of disobedience when

offenses rise high like tidal waves. Don't leave Him in timeout, huddled in a corner until you become religious. Take God with you. Take Him with you intentionally, exposing your truest self to Him and allowing that self to learn the truest things about Him.

Be friends with God. Walk with Him. Work for Him and with Him. Wrestle constantly; it keeps you in shape. Get mad and question. Stomp your feet if you have to. Shake your fist. Grieve. Do whatever you need to do in this lifetime to seek the truth at all cost. Do not live a counterfeit life. Matter.

Every once in a while, I smell sewage. Something in the wall down the pipes reminds me that there is a system by which all of our waste is eliminated. For some reason, no one smells it but me. As soon as I draw it to my husband's attention the scent dissipates, and he looks at me as if my imagination has got the best of me.

I can't explain why I'm the only one who detects the smell. All I can do is resolve within me that it exists. The reality is that every single one of us has a sewage system within us. If we don't take care of our business, it can overflow into other parts of the body. But when we come clean with God, you'd be surprised at how even the most unsavory processes can bring great relief. Even a ray of light in another person's universe. Remember, manure makes grass grow. Cycle of life. Period.

Live life honestly. Live enough to be compared to The Velveteen Rabbit. If you've never read that childhood book, make plans to. You need it. Let them know that your soul has been spray painted permanently in this place.

The author of the autobiography I read lived to beat the cancer—at least long enough to meet his son and finish the book. But he wrote like he wouldn't.

Homeless

Somewhere along the way, in my walk with God, I stopped attaching to things. I remember loving to shop. Every pay period I set aside some money and took myself shopping. Sometimes I forget how much I relished finding the perfect deal, the ideal fit, just the right bag, or something that would make my apartment spring to life.

I wasn't raised materialistic. Sure, we vacationed frequently and we ate out regularly, but in terms of shopping, my parents didn't believe in "buying just to buy." School shopping was one thing, but random splurging was another. Everything had a place and a purpose in our home.

Even when I started my first job, my money wasn't something to hold onto. It went into a savings account with the intent that it would reach a certain target. Whether the goal was paying for my driving permit, or saving for college books, in my family the point of working was to contribute your portion.

If I needed anything my parents provided it. And if I wanted something—well, did I ever really want anything? When did I stop wanting anything? The last time in my childhood that I wanted something was when I went Christmas shopping for my family.

My brother and I were given a certain amount of money to pool together to get gifts for everyone. I couldn't have been more than 11 years old. We were doing so well, when suddenly I saw a doll that stood up to my waist. I had never seen anything like it before. I needed her. I needed her so much that I bartered intensely with my brother.

So strategic, so targeted, was my argument that he—though two years younger than me, but twice as bright—succumbed. He looked at the doll and calculated the cost, then declared with conviction that if we bought the doll as his present for me, we would have just a few dollars left for everyone else.

I was blinded by greed. I couldn't rationalize soundly. I needed the doll. We got right up to the cash register when my inner turmoil surfaced. My brother was too good for me, and I was awful. I couldn't get the doll. It wasn't because I'd had a change of heart, nor had he convinced me otherwise. It was because, per usual, the maturity in me arrived just when I detested her the most. How would I face my parents?

I didn't get the doll when I wanted it. As I remember it, I walked away, but, perhaps I arrived at the car and my parents made me return it. Perhaps they showed up at the register and denied my request, or perhaps I couldn't afford it and purchased what I had chosen for everyone else.

Painstakingly I let it go. Funny enough, that Christmas I did get the doll, but for some reason the desire had passed. Dolls were a fleeting fancy that year. I was more impressed with the typewriter. I probably purged my toy box of all such dolls by the time the summer ended, just prior to 7th grade.

I never again wanted anything as badly as I'd wanted that doll. I'm not sure what changed. All I know is, once I was able to not only write my stories, but to see them become serious words typewritten on paper, nothing else was more worthy to hold onto than a word. A word was the only thing that could never, ever, be taken away from me. It was truly mine. I started to write when I was six years old. Ma and Pop, my great-grandparents, used to take care of me after school. I remember driving in the car with Pop on the way to the mall. I remember him stooping down to get a gumball from the candy machine for me. Even as an old man, Pop had an unparalleled vibrancy. And he knew stuff.

Pop worked with his hands, building things in the basement. And while building was his talent, he had earned his living, and then retired, as an elevator operator in the city. But truly, more than anything else, Pop was a writer. He never had his work published, and I grieve to this day that when he died I wasn't old enough to confiscate his writings for a day in which I could make him proud.

Pop read his stories to me. I not only listened, his words transformed me. My mom and dad were getting a divorce, and my brother and I shared a bed in my father's one bedroom flat on Dennis Street in Boston. Dad moved out of the family home, the one they had built, with the swingset in the perfect neighborhood where I adopted a cat and learned to ride a bike. They sold the house, displacing us all. I think I've been displaced ever since. At that young age, when my whole world was stolen from beneath my feet and my future was yet uncertain, this old man sewed a purpose in the hem of the garment of my soul. He read to me, and then one day, he sat me down with paper and a pencil and said, "Now you write."

I've spent most of my life homeless, but I've never been without a word to bring me home.

Restless Nights

Sometimes for no reason at all, I wake up restless in the middle of the night. It's as if an alarm goes off in me and nothing and nobody can keep me asleep. When this happens I've learned to give God His due.

There are times when God has something to say that you must hear and for some reason, no other time is right. Restless nights are reserved for coming to God with the firstfruits of your energy.

When I come, sometimes I read, sometimes I write or meditate. Always I listen. What am I listening for? A deep move. At these times, more than at others, when the world around me has come to a temporary stop, I can hear a movement in the spirit realm. While I've taught myself to do this at anytime and anywhere, even in times of duress, restless nights are best.

Deep calleth out to deep, the Scripture says.

What is it, my soul? What ails you? Why are you stirring, refusing to be comforted? What do you discern? What do you hear? What do you feel?

Often I am tempted to worry myself over news that comes to me about the demise of the world. Earlier in my career with God, it would distract me. But I've learned to push all other sounds out of my temple and concentrate on the only sound that matters, the whisper of God.

Lately I've been feeling something, an ominous brush stroke in my spirit, as if something has passed by me and we touched for a moment. A cold, dark, distant feeling that tempts me to worry about things I can't control. I've learned to take my concerns to the Lord and to wait on Him for my peace to return to me.

My husband and I bought a new dining room set today. The table is bar height with chairs that leave my feet dangling, but for him, at 6'4, the chair height is so natural. Finally, he can sit without his legs cramped up under the table.

What I like is that I can see out of our huge glass windows, farther than I previously could. I can see things in greater detail, without effort. But tonight I sit, with little light, trying hard to get this restless edge out of my soul, unable to see anything. Maybe I went to bed too early. I make excuses for this energy tantrum that refuses to find her resting place.

I gave up weighing myself. I'm on my last week stretch, and it was becoming a problem. Desperately needing to see change, wanting so bad to believe God for my full recovery, I watched the scale like a hawk. And no matter how many times He told me to focus on the act instead of the results, humanity judges the work by what it can see. Needing, wanting, desiring without reservation immediate results that prove that He is still with me—I worry. I worry against my will.

There's a nick in the new table. *Are you kidding me?* I color it in quickly with a dark pen. I don't want my husband to notice. I don't want him to have a reason to complain about the store we bought it from. My mother warned us about them, but I pressed. *Everybody's experience is different,* I told him.

My youngest son is avoiding me. He's taking too long to return my texts. When I call he lets it go to voicemail. I feel like he's floating. My husband tells me to let the children go. They are all adults, our Brady Bunch family, his three and my three. But I can't. I can't let them go. My failures haunt me; guilt consumes me. *Why am I here in DC, when I should be there where they are in Boston?* Even my son in California could find me if I had stayed.

I can't protect them from here. Then I remember that God sent me. I am where He wants me to be. The sadness is unbearable, though. I feel a conflict in my soul. What right do I have to have a life beyond all that I've ever known? What right do I have to live without grief? And there it is, in the center of my soul, keeping me up these restless nights: The devil wants me to stay in grief. He wants my life to be without joy. He wants to kill me before I have a chance to realize that I'm happy.

Quitter

I don't want to be married today. That's not unusual for me. I've been known to quit a thing or two. It's the idea of being stuck with a decision that bothers me. I hate having to live with a bad choice. The notion of staying with something just because at one time you chose to seems, I don't know—stupid—to me. But I'm not childish enough to ignore the obvious. You can't quit every time you wake up on the wrong side of the bed. Or can you?

I just got out of the shower and realized I forgot to get a fresh towel. Today was laundry day. I locked myself out of the apartment and put clothes in the dryer on the second floor, only to find out that the dryer on the second floor isn't working. Oh, and that kale

I've been devouring like a starved rabbit, hoping it would miraculously heal me, reveals itself to be an inflammatory and causes kidney stones when eaten raw. Even in small servings.

Yeah, apparently eating raw kale does some irreversible damage to your thyroid. Do I panic? No. It's one of those days. I've had them before, and so have you. But I know by now that when these days happen, it's best to ignore them, to put the dishwasher on, use paper plates for dinner and go to bed early.

Start fresh tomorrow. The reality is that life isn't supposed to be over just because you're having a bad day or a bad week, or even a bad month, quarter, season, or year. Even if you are having a bad life, you get no permission from God to quit. Life does not end for you until God says it does, and quite frankly, that sucks sometimes.

I look at people who've gone through catastrophic events and they don't seem to complain even half as much as I do, and I can't fathom why that is. I hate that I complain, not out loud of course, but in my heart. I want to be better. I want enough to be enough, but it never is. I hate that enough is never enough for me and that I'm rarely satisfied.

I hate that I need more out of life and that I feel like quitting when it seems like it's never going to change and God isn't helping me. But my curiosity gets the best of me and I don't want to go out like that. I want to know, gotta know, how it will end.

And so I wake up today, after yesterday seemed so bad, and I pat my husband on the butt. I love my husband. *Today I'm glad that I'm married.* I'm glad I'm married to him, my third husband, whom I feel God handpicked for me. I'm glad I married this man who holds me accountable to a standard. He is such a hard worker and a good provider, and I appreciate him. I appreciate him *especially* today, because it's been a hell of a week, and he's loved me through it. I'm discouraged in the pit of my soul, but it's Friday and it's over. I can breathe.

That's not to say that next week won't hold for me some hell of its own, but I've learned that this, too, will pass. I've learned that even a hellish year is required to give me periodic breaks. It may very well be my turn to experience hell again; it's been awhile. I've been enjoying the fruit of my labor. Along with some minor scrapes and bruises, life has given me a few sabbaticals. Maybe, just maybe, it's once again my turn to resist the devil until he flees from me.

As for today, I remember my refuge cities and I take cover in the Sabbath. I wake up this morning with pep in my step because I know that come hell or high water, it ends today for a minute. And truthfully, a minute is all I need to catch my breath.

I don't need to quit the same way anymore. I stopped quitting like that a decade ago. I stopped becoming burnt out, tired, exhausted and weary in well doing. I learned that God's system provides safe places for me to rest. I take advantage of the stop signs.

At this point in my life, the Sabbath is as important to me as air. I protect my breath, and I protect my Sabbath. I need it in order to step away from the rat race. The Sabbath gives me permission to remember that there is more to this life than nightly series, deadlines that can't be missed, and paperwork that must get in. There is the whisper of God in the air, the secret of life on the wings of time. It moves slowly, and I want to hear it.

I still quit, but not like I used to. Now, I quit at night when I can, and when I can't, I order my body to stop on Fridays, just before sundown. Shabbat Shalom!

Quest for the Perfect Orgasm

I once posted on a forum and got my feelings hurt. The debate was about men and women and the sexual tension between them. I went out on a limb when posting was new to me, and public opinion meant everything. I set aside my reservations and cast my thoughts on the line.

I said, "Maybe women are dissatisfied with their sexual experiences. Did you know that statistical data tells us that the majority of women don't have orgasms?"

Had the response been that they didn't believe me—these were men—I could handle that. A hearty debate has never scared me. Had the response been surprise, anger, sorrow, a need for understanding the female soul, I would have met it face-to-face, ready, willing, and able to engage in a lengthy discussion. But one lone ranger posted back a response that I will never forget: "Who cares!"

I, the daughter who was raised by a single father, the woman who takes pride in advocating fiercely for men, was amazed. *Maybe he misunderstood. Maybe he thinks that my comment was off topic. I can fix this,* I thought. But then he repeated the painful truth before I had time to poke the bear: "Who cares whether or not a woman has an orgasm?"

I have to pause here and tell you that we ended up becoming online friends in the course of debating back and forth until we both felt heard. However, I never forgot his initial comment because he spoke the words many men think, but would never say, and words many women accept, but would never admit. *Who cares about the woman?*

Well, God cares. Doesn't He count for anything? God cares about the woman. God cares that she has become an accessory rather than the partner she was designed to be. Why is it important for a woman to have an orgasm? Because without it, she doesn't know that she was not created as an afterthought; that she is not the dessert to his filet mignon. She is, in fact filet mignon herself, and possesses in her body a dessert all her own. If she doesn't know that, she can't fathom the depths to which God went in order to so brilliantly create and design her that she must be unlocked to truly be appreciated!

I was a young bride, no more than 20 years old when my brother

33333333333

called me from college. He was drunk at the time, so his ramblings were the norm. We are always so close and candid with one another. He had just been introduced to the topic of the female orgasm and was calling to inform me that most women will go their entire lives without experiencing one.

He ended the conversation—I was rushing him off of the phone—by making me swear an oath that I would look into this and take care of my own body. It was such a strange conversation. Most likely one he had forgotten fifteen minutes after he passed out that night. We never spoke of it again. His words, however, changed my life; they altered my thoughts of myself, and most importantly, my perspective of who I was in God's eyes.

I am not a sperm receptacle, designed solely to carry life for someone else, devoid of a life of my own. More women are dying, collapsing of heart disease in their forties than ever before, and I can't help but wonder if they ever even had the pleasure of a female ejaculation. To live your whole life and never experience the sweet fragrance of a cosmic release is to miss out on a precious secret that God designed just for you.

Who cares if the woman is so frustrated that she gets caught up in adultery? Who cares if the woman suffers for twelve years with an issue of blood? Who cares if her daughter is dying? Who cares if men have used, abused, dismissed, rejected, and abandoned her? Who cares about the woman?

When Eve wandered off from her husband, she found out that Satan knew who she was. He saw her restlessness and despair. But the snake had no power to release her. He could only highlight the problem, hoping she finds no solution.

The woman is a rare pearl tossed before swine. Somebody told her that nobody cares about the murmurs of her heart. They lied. Jesus cares.

CHAPTER TEN

Whol "*C*" Ness Protects Your Covenant

Tomorrow There's Sh*t To Do

At noon my husband and I will head to Virginia Beach. From DC it's a three-hour drive in moving traffic. My sister lives there now, but our main purpose is to check on his 92-year-old grandmother. My husband is a natural born caretaker. He is a provider and a protector. He can't help himself.

Aside from our vacation to Boston, this is the only weekend that he's had off since we got married. But even on a weekend that doesn't require rising at 5:00 in the morning, he is compelled to do something productive. I try to convince him that the Sabbath is important. He agrees to this quickly, and then moans that his salary doesn't support taking weekends off yet.

I shake my head. This way of thinking is backwards. There will always be something that needs to be done. I try to convince him to keep the Sabbath even if that means lost wages and projects that go undone. The conversation is fruitless, partly because my husband has graciously given me a year off. Because I don't work outside of the home, I really have no leg to stand on. He is doing the work of two so that he can support us while I write and take care of my body.

He agreed to this as part of our marital arrangement. I literally said, "I'm in no position to get married right now. I need to take a year to get myself together." He promptly responded, "I can do that. I can give you a year off. Stay home, take time to yourself, and write your book."

I looked at him in disbelief, but he has kept his word. The spoiled child in me wonders why all things can't be done at the same time. Why does my husband have to work so much? Why do I have to work at all? Can't both lives coexist? The answer is simple. *Because there is sh*t to do.* I hate that in my immaturity I just can't seem to appreciate the concept, that sh*t has to be done, because that's no way to live.

Sh*t simply isn't that important. Why do we waste our whole lives trying to accomplish it. What meaning is there in the mundane—getting up, hustling for another dollar, only to hand it over to pay your car note? I'm such a free bird, a gypsy, a flower child, a Gemini. I walk around with my sun-kissed skin and blonde hair that gets even lighter when I spend my days slipping into the chlorine-filled pool. I'm immature to be sure. I stop to pick the daisies, and I stop to smell the roses. Like my mom, who taught me the gift of appreciating the simplicities of a simple life, I worry about nothing. Well, I worry about nothing financially—in this season.

Several years back, after the twin towers saw their demise, I decided I wasn't wasting my life on the sh*t that needed to be done. I was the managing director at an executive search boutique in downtown Boston. My office overlooked Faneuil Hall. Prior to that I was the assistant vice president of executive search at a major financial institution. I walked every day, even in the snow, from South Station.

One day, as my first marriage began to show public signs of crumbling, I looked out of the large windows that overlooked all that mattered to everyone else, and I said to myself, "*There may be sh*t to do, but surely this can't be it.*"

Summer Camp: Don't Be Without Understanding

If you really understood how clever our enemy is, you'd never rejoice again over the fallen who stood as beacons of light for your welfare. I hate it when those who attend church, rarely, seldom, or never, criticize those who attend faithfully. I don't mind when unbelievers do it. They actually have a right, for we are supposed to set an example. We are supposed to be a lighthouse beckoning them to come home. But when believers who decided that they were better off without the Church stand and point weaponry at the Lord's anointed it goes right through me.

If you think that believers are supposed to be flawless, you're going to have to throw out the Bible. Only One was perfect. Only One. The rest of us, brandished with the scarlet letter, are sinners, saved by *grace*, working out our salvation—however poorly—daily. We suck at it, and we are already aware. So, no thanks for keeping the scoreboard.

When I was young, I always went to camp. Sometimes there were day camps, and sometimes there were overnight camps. I always complained. The idea of camp is far less appealing than what you'll remember about it as you age (providing it was a safe camp).

At camp I was exposed to things I never would have been otherwise. I played tennis and learned to swim like a lifeguard. I water-skied and went horseback riding. And though I never truly appreciated some of the activities, like archery or arts and crafts, they had their place, I later learned. The purpose of camp is exposure. It's to provide choices that might otherwise never cross a child's mind. I often look at kids today who spend their summer hooked on video games, either sweltering or shivering indoors. I shake my head with compassion. *How can you know the choices you have, if you've never been presented with them?*

Church is the campsite. It's the place where the privileged and the underserved gather to learn what may never be presented to them in any other forum. It's where we gather to encourage one another, correct one another, and learn to hear others' opinions. If you were lucky enough to attend since childhood, church is where you learned to respect and honor what's holy. Not to say that, perhaps like with archery or arts & crafts, you'll never return to the things you learned—but at least you won't say you never had the education or the introduction.

It was at church that you first started networking, and compromising, and serving people who were not your family. It's the first corporation you ever worked for. You learned how to dress for a job interview before you even knew what a job was, and you learned how to sit still for a lecture, before you ever signed up for your first seminar.

Like everything, church has its place. It may or may not be the place where you first meet God—truly meet Him. But it is definitely the place where you've rubbed elbows with some who did. Coming in contact with their anointing changed the course of your life without you ever knowing it. So when we snobbishly turn our noses up to the very assembly, putting a hand up against the ones who held us down, this is not good.

One of the first things we learn in camp is team-building skills. We come outside of ourselves. We wear the same color t-shirts and we chant and pound tables until we make everyone understand that our team is a force to be reckoned with. We jump in the pool with all of the other campers, recognizing that we are all there for the same reason. Not because we are athletic, or smart or ambitious—but because our parents signed us up. Our parents knew that camp would offer us a way out… and stop us from thinking that what we currently knew was enough. Yes, some campers are obnoxious, but what of all the pretty horses?

Stick to the Plan

If you don't have a plan, you won't discern a move of God that alters it. You will think that every movement is whimsical, or spontaneous, when nothing could be further from the truth. I'm tired today. Very tired. I power walked while on some herbal liquid that's supposed to cleanse your innermost parts. And it's working. Well, who knows if it's truly working—it could be just purging out stuff that doesn't matter.

Faith lies dormant in the belly of the believer until we decide that something or someone has earned our allegiance. Yesterday I felt remorse over an affair I had, once upon a time. I looked at my body in the mirror, and I was disgusted. Not disgusted with my body per se, but disgusted by my inability to help her. For some reason, the feelings that surfaced—insecurity, inadequacy, and insufficiency—made me reflect on the affair. I didn't think of the man I thought I was in love with, instead I thought of his wife, whom I clearly had not considered before. Nor had I considered her this way.

As I looked at my body, I was flooded with all of the memories of the conversations we had.

"Did he tell you that he has two small children?"

"Yes."

I wondered how many times she looked at her reflection, feeling inadequate, insecure, and inefficient. She probably tried to hold her stomach in. Undoubtedly she dabbed on some makeup to cover the eyes swollen from tears spilled the night before. She fidgeted with her hair; of course, it never came out quite right. Rolls of stubborn fat became more noticeable, previously hidden cellulite now visible and unbearable. What happened to the definition in my arms? She scowled. But breakfast had to be made, bills had to be paid; she had no time to grieve over her own dissatisfaction. Soon she criticized her fading wardrobe, and the small house was never clean enough. She wasn't smart enough, clever enough, witty enough, pretty enough. Had she been all of those things, maybe—just maybe—he wouldn't have wanted somebody else.

I had been a wife before. I had been a mistress. Neither side is that impressive. As women, we are not enough. We will never reach the standard set for us. We are not feminine enough, strong enough, or ageless enough. We will always be compared to youth, to wisdom, to monuments. There is no room to be flawed.

I once heard a man say that he couldn't understand how his wife could forgive his indiscretion because he wouldn't forgive her. And that settles it, right there. Women are not worthy of forgiveness.

I contacted her, the wife. It's been many years now. The domino effect of my affair with her husband has inevitably infected every fabric of her household. Things changed because of me. I could smell it because I had lived it before, myself.

I can't rewrite the past. Nothing that I do now will ever take away the pain of the betrayal I participated in. All I could do was take ownership for my part. I am remorseful. I asked for her forgiveness. Time doesn't heal all wounds. Sometimes wounds become worse over time. Sometimes they scar over and cause future problems. No, time doesn't heal all wounds. God heals all wounds.

I felt a remnant of something in my foot. It was either glass or a stone. I was too busy to deal with it. I accommodated the pain by just avoiding certain shoes. Over time I walked with a limp.

Recently my husband insisted, impressing upon me the urgency of dealing with the issue. I dug it out early one Saturday morning. Relieved, I couldn't fathom why I hadn't dealt with it sooner.

The Tone of DC

Just like guys want girls to be unrealistically feminine, girls want guys to be unrealistically masculine. Doesn't leave much room for the truth. If men were truly masculine they'd have no need for women, and if women were truly feminine, what would they have in common with men? We need this entangled chemistry. It's what attracts us to one another. Without it, everyone would turn to their own kind and children would be either nonexistent or relegated to our "to do" list. Too much masculinity and too much femininity cause us to steer clear of one another. Self-consumed and fascinated by our own gender and agenda, there is no space for the complexity of real men and women.

Kissing, I've been told is for women. Yet without it, men do not become emotionally attached to their mates, and women don't see men as irreplaceable. The kiss tells us what we need to know about a person. You may know everything you need to know, but until you've experienced the kiss, *you don't know enough.*

A city can be like that. It beckons you to read about it, to visit its museums, frequent its restaurants, taste its mimosas. There is an advantage to being a tourist. But you only see what they want you to see. You haven't kissed the city until you've lived there.

As a child I experienced Washington, DC on television. Anything that was anything happened in Washington, DC or Arlington, Virginia. It was the hub of real life drama spread sensationally across newspapers and modern day media. DC has a Hollywood of its own, save the year round sunshine and the big white letters. We have The White House. Nothing else to say after that.

DC is less impressive once you're in it, not because you're not impressed, but because the struggle becomes real. Down the street from the Oval Office, a man comes into a Chinese food restaurant that seats at most six at a time. It's mainly take-out. He approaches my husband, but before he can say a word my husband answers him. No matter how badly the man wants to be heard, my husband isn't buying it. What he is buying is some food for the man, even though my husband knows instinctively that the man didn't come for food.

My husband has been kissed by the District since childhood. Born and raised here, he has an advantage over me. I'm a tourist. It doesn't matter how long I live here, or how much I think I hear from the streets, I never hear quite as clearly as I would, had I been a native.

I compare DC to my hometown. Riddled with crime and desperately trying to maintain its place on the map, it sinks further and further from the Hollywood version we all like to believe.

Wasn't it exciting when I visited four years ago with my son? Didn't we see everything? Doesn't my son still wear the baseball cap I bought him on the street, near The White House—the same street I live on now?

I haven't been kissed by DC yet. I haven't been kissed, but I suspect his tongue is smooth. I suspect he is practiced: a mixture of experience and uncertainty. Tentative, as if he isn't sure he remembers how to do it. It's been so long since a kiss meant anything. The streets have forgotten romance. Boasting of high profile positions and competitive salaries that still land you in the poorhouse. Everyone is trying to be someone in DC. Culturally rich with religion, spiritually dry as a famine. The city has lost touch with God, lost touch with women, lost touch with the act of surrender. The tone is masculine, but not in the way we remember. Not masculine for the purpose of covering, caring for, protecting and providing. The city hasn't kissed me, though my husband has.

On The Down Low

I blew it, Lord. Where do I go from here?
Man, if we could only profess that more often. Perhaps the turnaround time would be a lot quicker. Being a woman is one of the

most complicated jobs on the face of the planet. Blessed with the qualifications for the #1 spot, you're hired for the #2 position.

And if that isn't insulting enough, there's an epidemic of married men who are privately seeking the company of other men—and I don't mean for golf. I have to ask myself, what pleasure they are getting out of it that they wouldn't get from a woman—if in fact, they married a woman in the first place. But, after doing much research and opening my heart for the purpose of getting a glimpse of understanding, I realized what has happened.

The reality is, no one really likes women. That's tragic. Women require too much, they are too challenging to love, they aren't beautiful enough, and they aren't toned enough. They need surgery to stay youthful looking, hair extensions to be desirable, fake lashes, fake breasts, fake butts. Liposuction here, facelift there, and at the end of the day, they will be dismissed and replaced by a younger version who doesn't mind being cast for the lead role in a porn video.

This is what we are left with, God's cherished daughters. Then they wonder why we grow old badly, grow bitter sooner, angry as hell, vengeance in heels. Men who know these women decide that it's easier to deal with another man. Not truly homosexual, they just want a quick fix with no complications. This is what I've read. A quick fix with no complications—yup. That doesn't sound like a woman, not one you've married anyway. She may be one you've dated or continue to date; either way, she has no real vested interest in you.

But if you marry her, she becomes the woman who will drive you into the car of another man. Why? Because behind closed doors, women are human. When the angel wings come off and the weave has seen a better day; when the stretch marks show, and the wrinkles give way, the man is faced with the worst kind of truth. He never *loved* the woman.

Maybe She's Born With It, Maybe It's Maybelline

I have no desire to be young again. I never truly valued anything that was given to me for free. Truth is, I don't even want to look young again. What I want is to look good. What I want is for my hard work to be manifested, not just in my outer appearance, but also in my inner health. I want what I deserve. Not the bad things, of course. Nobody wants those. For those days, I'll take the Maybelline. I want what I was born with, but I also want the fruit of my labor.

My husband frustrated me today. He wanted me to take care of some things, and in fairness to him, I had said that I would. However, something came up—*me*. I realized after coming home from vacation that I had gotten so preoccupied with my health—or lack thereof—that I had been neglecting those things that were most important to me. In my effort to hear my body, I pushed all other matters aside. I'm not saying that was bad. At the time it was the way I felt things had to be handled. It was, in my eyes, necessary—crucial. When it became clear that taking care of my health was gonna be awhile, I began to realize that I can't stop living in the meantime.

I had loads of stuff on my desk. Everything believed itself to be a priority in my life, and my husband was no different. Pulling on me, unwilling to wait, unwilling to let me manage my own workload.

Finally, he took a project back from me and determined to do it himself. It was then that it occurred to me, *what am I afraid of? Am I afraid that he will see me without makeup? Will he realize I'm not the perfect flawless wife he wished he had married?*

I needed his help.

Maybe I've been treating God the same way. Some things I really was born with, but some things I've had to work hard for. On tired days, when I've given all that I can give and I need a moment to myself, you will see what I was born with, and what I plainly was not. Thank God He promised to cover me.

CHAPTER ELEVEN

Whole "*E*" Ness Protects *YOU!*

The Good Wife

*J*don't want to swim today, and I'm not sure why. Maybe my physical insecurities are creeping back again. Maybe it's not hot enough. Maybe I'm content. Maybe I'm bored.

There's a young man who looks to be my oldest son's age, who stares at me when he thinks I'm not looking. This makes it worse.

Why do we have to wear clothes? Why do we have to wear bodies?

I can tell what my husband is thinking when he goes to hug me or kiss me.

Is this ever going to end? Will the swelling ever be gone, or is this her new body?

What if this new sick, swollen body is my reproach for all that I've done, all that I've thought, all that I've thought about doing? Maybe God has taken away the temptation.

Maybe my marriage is being tested.

Can we love each other without lust? Can I love myself without being the woman I am used to being? Who am I if the sex appeal is gone? What do I have to offer? What do I bring to the table, if all that made me alluring is stripped from me?

In the midst of my thoughts, I suddenly have this overwhelming urge to swim, to own my body again without apology.

What is this in me trying to bust out? And will I give into it?

I want to wear a sign that says: "Don't judge me. I eat well and exercise regularly, but I'm sick against my will. There is no cure because no one but God knows what's really wrong."

If I jump in, if I swim, then what? What's next?

Not so proud anymore. I can't help but wonder if Kendrick Lamar's song was meant for me. *Sit down, b*tch, be humble.* Who is humbling me? What do I do to get out of the glitch I'm stuck in? Should I never see myself as sensual and sexy and beautiful again? Should I never boast about the work I've put in getting my body in shape? Is that the secret? Or is there really no lesson here?

Is it just one of those things that I'm destined to live with because I'm human and this is how it goes? I wish I could give up. I hate myself for not giving up. It takes so much time and energy to desire to be the perfect woman for a man who deserves to be loved by her, but I'm not perfect.

Permission Granted

What if God gave you permission to do what you needed to do, no holds barred? Would the assignment be nearly as intoxicating?

My apartment complex has a nice sized pool. A baby is wandering around unattended. We all watch, waiting for the moment when we are needed because his caregiver isn't paying attention.

We manage other people better than we do ourselves. We care about their success, or lack thereof, whether our motives are pure or not. What is it that makes us so consumed with other people's business? Perhaps it's the ability to give your input without taking any genuine responsibility.

When we determine to care for the business that has been given to us we become different people. We become better. I know that I'm guilty of this. I am the quintessential support person, designated catcher of dropping pieces.

I wasn't always like this. Fear crept into the crevices of my work—and I know exactly when it happened.

See, when I was carnal, excelling based on luck or chance, it was easier. I was dumber and the world was a better place. What I didn't know wasn't hurting me. I took chances because I was invested in this world. I cared deeply about how well I prospered in it.

Then, I came into a saving knowledge of Jesus Christ. I'm not going to lie to you—it was the worst thing that ever happened to me. Walking with God confused everything. My priorities changed. I could no longer think clearly because the logic line had been moved. My objectives were suddenly supernatural. I couldn't measure them by worldly standards.

As a result, I was lost. I never quite got my bearing back. How do you recover from a hit to your universe? I began to think like angels and yes, even demons, and that was okay. What was not okay was having to juggle a supernatural life with a natural life. Living as Clark Kent and Superman has its drawbacks. How can you ever convince yourself that average work is appealing after scaling tall buildings in a single bound? It's easier to stare at the baby and hope that he doesn't drown.

Don't Eat Eggs

So, a few years ago they said that they found the secret to good health. Stay away from eggs. Eggs are bad for cholesterol.

Feverishly everyone took cover. Why didn't I think of that? Folks abandoned eggs in droves and the price of eggs skyrocketed. The same went for salt, and then bread.

I laughed beside myself when my grandfather reminded me of how he doesn't use salt. I politely—okay, not so politely—pointed to the chips. "And these are better?"

He smiled. Everything is relative.

Skip the healthy banter and cut to the chase. It isn't the eggs, the bread, or even the salt that's killing us. It's what we've decided to substitute in their place, all in the name of becoming healthy. We still sneak chips and cookies and frappes, but we swear off the things that have been around since the beginning of time. What sense does that make?

Wouldn't it be simpler—just saying—to see the camel and stop straining at the gnat? We do the same thing in our lives and in our faith walk with God.

I once said, "Men should skip opening the car door and just come home at night." I was kidding, sort of. We live in a culture where only how everything looks matters, from designer handbags to having a husband who is flagrantly gay, but at least he pays the bills.

Quick fixes and façades have become so much of an epidemic that we can't even discern when the health community is selling a crock of bull. There are no shortcuts. Sacrificing eggs and salt and bread will not excuse the chocolate cake and beer and tootsie rolls, no matter how much we ignore the obvious. The fact remains and the truth prevails.

But I have to wonder if my generation has tired of the truth. Perhaps we no longer want it to be plain as day. Perhaps a riddle is better. Dubner Maggid once said, "Truth was walking down the street stark naked, but he had to be dressed in a parable because no one could stand the sight of him." Maybe that's why we love movies—we never have to see ourselves naked because the story is always about somebody else.

I had a colleague who used to order a diet coke and a piece of chocolate cake for lunch. He told me they canceled each other out. Well, at least he doesn't eat eggs.

The Solution Was Given, But We Will Conveniently Forget

Why is it that we never remember the still, small voice? Elijah had come to the end of himself. He was exhausted. He fought the good fight, but at the end of the day, courage had failed, stamina was gone and all resolve had taken the next plane back to Boston. It was too much for him. The great prophet had met his match.

What was so intimidating about Jezebel? Well, for starters, they both wanted the same thing: what was best for Ahab. The problem was that Elijah was hired to deliver what was best for God; and that required that Elijah take one for the team. Have you ever been there?

It takes a certain kind of person to take one for the team. It's the kind of person who is able to put their own interests aside for the greater good of everyone else. I'm not like this, but God is training me to be.

When the Israelites spied out Canaan, they were thinking about themselves, *not* the nation that God was creating in their children. Elijah, on the other hand, was smart enough to hold his tongue until he was in the right place. He sought sanctuary, literally. In fact, he ran until he got there. Elijah didn't infect anyone with his thoughts, though he was desiring to die, that's how discouraged he was. He waited until he could get space with God.

What was God able to do for Elijah that he couldn't do for himself? God was able to show up. The old-timers used to say, "All I need is a little talk with Jesus." They weren't kidding. Elijah had to get as far away from his own voice as possible.

Have you ever been there—where you knew you had to get as far away from *you* as you could? And I mean quickly? A place where a hurricane would drown out your own opinion, a tornado would blow away your own solutions, a place where you couldn't hear anything else you had to say? Yes, that place. That's where Elijah ran.

After the elements beat down his own inclination toward self-preservation, he heard what he had always known.

What are you doing here?

When God shows up, he will clear away the cobwebs in your brain. Elijah answers, like any person would, with the complaints of his heart. But God asks him the same question again, and Elijah hears it in a different tone.

What was your assignment?

And now Elijah is stuck. He's stuck because he has a choice. Do I take the splinter out, or do I leave it in there. There are consequences to both. Elijah has come face to face with the truth and it isn't pretty.

"I can't do it."

Elijah runs all the way to the sanctuary to find refuge in God. His soul is driving him to the mercy seat.

"Lord, I've failed you. Lord, this is too hard for me. Lord, I have no solution."

And suddenly it comes to him, there in the presence of the Most High. The solution was clear all along. All he needed was a circuitous route.

You can do it. Just do it differently.

How many times have we ever considered that God gives us the *grace* to accomplish what He has commissioned us to do? And how many times have we overlooked what having His *grace* truly means? It means we have permission to do it by whatever means necessary. The solution was clear all along. He didn't come into the sanctuary looking for a solution. He came begging for permission to execute it his way.

Unexpected Things

Early every morning, before the sun was evident to everyone else, my stepmother was up. She came into my life when I was 8 and married my father when I was 12. She helped my father raise my brother and me. A good part of who I've become can be attributed to her home training.

My father, who was always a disciplinarian, relaxed his rod of correction once she entered the scene. Raising children took on an entirely different tone. Instead of being vagabonds who relied heavily on love, loyalty and Dinty Moore stew—with ketchup—we became an established family.

My father previously treated my brother and me like comrades, but my stepmother swiftly revised our roles and taught us how to think, behave, and appreciate the perks of childhood. Sometimes this was confusing because I had been an adult for so long. I allowed her love, and oftentimes her temper, to mold me into a different kind of person than I would have been without her. She, more than anyone in my life, taught me and continues to teach me what it means to take one for the team.

In my world with Dad, though the three of us were destined to be pals for a lifetime in fantasyland, we had set up an unrealistic universe. In that universe, nobody would ever leave and nobody would ever grow up. You can see how eventually that might be a problem.

My stepmother snatched me from that universe, sometimes with brute strength, and forced me to live outside of the circle the three of us created. It was painful and many times I disagreed with her strategy that seemed to tear me away from my position in Dad's life as daddy's girl. I protested vehemently, at times throwing childish tantrums, but she took it. Somehow she knew that my Dad had become a god to me.

Not only was I blind to his imperfections, I refused to see his frailties and often thought that he could save me perpetually. This bad habit I had of needing my father's salvation became a crutch in my adult years, crippling my ability to separate from him, and preventing me from taking ownership, authority, and accountability over my own decisions.

On the one hand, being so close to my father was a rarity in my generation. For a black woman to be raised not only with, but *by* her father was an anomaly. But on the other hand, I desperately needed his approval and affirmation over my life in an unhealthy way. I needed him to validate my decisions, when in many cases, he could not.

The thought of losing my place in my father's eyes devastated me. I couldn't reconcile who I was if I wasn't Daddy's girl. His shadow covering me made me feel as if I could do anything.

Slowly, my stepmother snipped the flesh of the umbilical cord that kept me attached to my father. I hated her. I was angry and bitter, finding every reason to resent her and disavow all that she had sacrificed in order to ensure that my brother and I, as well as our children, excelled.

One day, when I had grown to be a woman, we came head to head and I told her that we should just stop trying. It was obvious that she would never be my mother, and I could never be her daughter. Our relationship was arduous, filled with sarcasm, awkward politeness and long bouts of silence. I thought for sure, once the pretense was over, we would drift apart. I expected it, and I was prepared for it.

What I wasn't prepared for was that the love that grew between the cement cracks of our relationship took on a mission of its own. I will always be a daddy's girl. But my stepmother put me there. I was in danger of becoming his wife, forfeiting a husband of my own, and she saw it ahead of time.

What If This Is Good News?

What if the bad report is good news? What would that change? The way we see everything of course!

The Israelites brought back a bad report when God told them to bring back the good news. They were so busy leaning on their own understanding that they never realized they had been duped.

Did God not know that they had been duped? Did God not know that there was a bad report? Did He not know that there was more bad than good, more problems than solutions, and more ailments than remedies? Did He not know?

If He did, why would He send them into the Promised Land and show them all that they could never conquer? I have an idea. Because their children were watching.

God wanted their children to pay attention to something in particular—and we are the children. When God sends you on an assignment, pay careful attention to what He says is the objective, because for sure, you will get distracted once you get there.

The spies saw the size of the people and dismissed the size of the fruit. They saw the fierceness of the warriors, instead of the expansion of the land. They saw what the adversary wanted them to see—the facts. And they completely forgot what God wanted them to obtain—the truth.

All they had to do was to confirm the truth. The truth was that God had not lied. That's it. That's it! That alone was enough to rejoice about.

When I think about living in DC, I laugh. I was designed for it. It was designed for me. It is correctly referred to as a district. A district of what? An angle, a corner, a slice of every kind of specimen in the nation. It harbors the elite versus the impoverished, the highly educated versus the elementary school dropout. In the corner of exhibits and the corner of exhibitionists, they live together as neighbors, down the street from one another.

On 16th street where I power walk daily, it looks as if the Ivy Leaguers set up camp. "Good morning—Good morning," we greet each other. One way leads to Maryland, the other directly to the White House, and I am at home here. Did I not grow up in a suburban town in Massachusetts? Did I not learn how to manicure a lawn, walk a dog, and be polite to strangers? Yes I am at home here, able to hob knob with politicians and lobbyists. I was born for this street. I wear it well.

But some mornings I take a right outside of my door and I bypass 16th Street. I cross over the comfort of my suburban roots and I make my way to Georgia Avenue where Family Dollar has bars on the windows and Walmart has no Caucasian face in plain sight. I realize that I am also at home here.

I was prepared for this. Didn't I spend the greater part of 30 years of my life in the inner city? Fighting crime, homelessness, and helplessness? It's familiar to me. I'm not afraid here. I'm at home in DC.

And yet when God commissioned me to go, first by a gnawing in my stomach, and then with a tap on the shoulder, and finally with a *rhema* word, I was prepared to bring Him back a bad report.

They are too sophisticated. They are too impoverished. They are too cosmopolitan. They are too ghetto.

But I realized that everything I would have said about them was everything they could have said about me. Suddenly I have understanding. Wasn't it true? The land was me, and I am her.

Did God lie when He sent me? No. God did not lie. This is my district, my corner, my angle, and my piece of the world. For in the bad report there was good news. I am a fierce warrior. I am a giant people. I am good fruit and an expansive land.

They failed to see what God saw. God saw Israel there. Unfortunately, when we don't see ourselves as we are, we miss out on the good news: You're home. Confirm that you are.

Part Two

Behold, All Things Are New

CHAPTER TWELVE

Whol "$\mathcal{E}$" ness Protects Your CORE

A Dedicated Time

*W*hy didn't the leaders take the time to bring their concerns before God? They were grieving enough to stop talking to God, grieving enough to stop going forward, grieving enough to take it to the down low. Why didn't the leaders confess to God their dirty, dark little secret, that they were human: that they had needs that weren't being met? Deep, deep, way down deep in the soul needs. Even though they were grieving, didn't they have a social responsibility to keep it real?

Maybe they didn't tell God because they knew, maybe because they thought they knew what He would say, or maybe because they didn't want to take the time. Maybe, just maybe, though they grieved, they didn't have time to talk to God because there was too much "sh*t" to do.

See, when we really want to petition God, nothing else can be on the table. All other distractions must be pushed aside. Never mind the calendar or the schedules. Put aside the budgets and the accounts. Forget for a moment the staff and the clients. Neglect the systems and consecrate a time in between times. A time when the grieving has stopped and before all the "sh*t to do" gets done. Consecrate a season to petition God, for joy.

The only way out of grief is to produce joy. So we come to God the best way we know how, humbly, on our knees, with our faces towards the rising Son, and we beg Him to have mercy on us. A people, covered by the shadow of the Most High God, are ashamed to confess that what they presently have, even being the very Elect, is not enough. They need more. We need more. We need to produce something that we can't possibly produce without *Him*.

And He answers us when we least expect it. The answer is not miraculous, the way we had hoped. It doesn't happen overnight the way we wished it would. Instead, it requires work. We have 10 objectives that we must meet before the womb of our soul can birth what is required in order for us to step out of our grieving garb.

We must:

1. Mimic the life of Christ
2. Understand that mimicking means copying
3. Know that copying Jesus demands change
4. Accept that change has a cost
5. Be willing to die, and dying requires a time of dedication

Did you catch that? Before we can even go any further we must be willing to die. We come to God dedicated to dying. Dying to what? Dying to our own will. In the middle of our petition, before the last five objectives are set out, we must first leave our own will at the altar, on the cross, in His hands.

The tone of the last five objectives changes because you change. You change before you even change. It may be your will to grieve. You may have every right to grieve, but you are willing to change on His call. Changing on the very call of God is your moral, corporate, and social responsibility. You must change, despite how you feel.

What separates the seed of Isaac from the seed of Ishmael is their mothers. Ishmael's mother cried out, and God heard her. But

Isaac's mother, though she was grieving, heard God. One is the petitioner, the other is the receiver. Sarah conceived Isaac not because she was no longer grieving. She conceived Isaac even though she was grieving, because it was the will of God, and she accepted it.

"How long will you grieve over Saul, knowing that I have rejected him?" God asks Samuel when Samuel is devastated over the mistakes of the one he anointed. But God does not leave it there. He says to Samuel, "Arise and anoint the one that I will show you."

It was the decision to rise up and follow through with God's will that changed everything. Samuel didn't feel better when he went to Jesse's house. He didn't feel better when he examined all of Jesse's sons. I doubt he even felt better when the mantle was placed on David. But I do know this—I know that he decided to do the will of the One who sent him.

Joy springs from the decision to go forward, believing in the word of the One who sent you. Jesus bowed His head and died. He took His grief with Him to the grave, literally. But He trusted the Father, and found joy at the end of the follow through.

And so we decide to cross over. We decide to see our lives from a different perspective. We decide to hang our grief on yesterday. We decide to step into tomorrow.

> 1. Change your clothes: Be willing to let go of your old name, "The One Who Grieves" and the character that was attached to it. Take on the new name that has been prepared for you, "The One Who Rejoices." No longer will you be called, "The one who lives a life worth grieving about." Now you will be called, "Honest: The one who lives the truth worth rejoicing over."

> 2. Take a new character: Be willing to trust God with the future, the good seasons and the tough ones. Trust Him with the end results, always.

3. Do new things: Be willing to be flexible with the plan that God has for you. That new plan entails complete transparency with your Savior. Tell Him the truth, no matter how stinky it smells.

4. Stretch: New things are unfamiliar. Be willing to be pulled out of your comfort zone.

5. Grow: We become new creatures in Christ. Stretching means growing. Don't be afraid of who you are becoming. Don't be afraid of who you once were. Use it to the glory of God in order to tell your story. Don't be afraid anymore to be real.

One day, the season of grieving will cease, and you will experience your season of joy. Don't forget. The most dangerous thing we can do is to forget. When we forget, we stop being able to relate to the struggles of the next generation.

No matter how good you become at walking with God, remember there will always be room for improvement. It was at the height of his success that King David made his gravest mistakes.

Never get so comfortable in righteousness that you forget your humanity. Believe me when I tell you, only the bold record their sins for all the world to see.

"Everyone has their 'Lord have mercy.'"

-Elma Lewis

EPILOGUE
Rise & Shine and Give God *YOUR* Glory!

J was sitting with my youngest son today, shooting the
breeze. I spent a week in the three-family house with a
large apartment on the second floor that he and my daughter share as roommates. She made a spare bedroom for me out of
what used to be the nursery before my Boston grandbaby outgrew
it. We sat talking about my book, his music, and of course, God. It
seems that all of the conversations I have with my children eventually make their way back to the underlying theme of all stories: The
lifetime struggle with God. Try as we might to deviate from that
topic, to engage in conversations that intentionally exclude Him,
perhaps to make our own meager existence more relevant, it doesn't
work. Of course we are left back where we began. Life without
God is boring, meaningless, not worth whispering about. And so
He forces Himself upon us. Not in a hurricane or a tornado, but
in a still, small voice in the back of your mind, in the pit of your
stomach, until He stays on the tip of your tongue. The truth is, we
realize together, my son and I, that there is only one explanation
that makes sense. All of the "sh*t" that we have to do, all that we
ever had to do, woven between the fabric softener, rubbing itself
against the ever expanding bags of laundry, there in the milk carton
and the eggs, and in the 9 to 5 job you don't even remember the
name of now, but seemed so important when you had to hustle to
catch the train, has a purpose. There, right there, in the busy work

of "sh*t to do," He deserves the glory. That stuff that seems like nothing to me because I've never been a traditionalist and cubicles make me break out in hives, that nothingness, in all of it, even in the grief, He was there. What I disrespectfully call "sh*t" suddenly transforms itself in my "Aha" moment while I talk to my youngest son. All of that "sh*t" that I have to do is the life I am destined to live in order to display my gratitude.

In the mundane and the monotony, in the laughter and the euphoria, I owe God. I owe Him the glory. I owe Him the praise for waking me up this morning. I owe Him the honor for having my back when I wasn't looking over my shoulder. I owe Him the respect and the dignity of loving the life that He gave me.

We rode through McDonald's to each get a Mocha Frappe: the drink I swore I would never drink again when I realized it was responsible for most of my fat days. My quick-witted son said something funny, and I smiled—well, kind of cackled, apparently clearing a passageway in my throat and releasing mucus that probably needed to come out much earlier, but I was to too delicate to notice.

Out of nowhere, never before in my 49 years of living had I experienced snot shooting out of my nose and onto my pants, but there it was. Humiliating.

My son said, "I hope that was gum."

We exchanged hard glances.

"Was it?"

"Yes," I responded without hesitation.

My son looked at me intensely and in that moment the reality of who I was hit him.

"It wasn't gum, was it?"

I couldn't lie.

"No."

Suddenly, I laughed until tears poured from my eyes. It was

hysterical. The whole thing was hilarious to me. The very thought that he had no idea that I was human until that moment filled me with delight, a tickle I cannot explain, except to call it joy. Yes, there was joy. Earnest joy. Produced from something so utterly carnal.

Every morning when they were growing up, despite my hidden grief, I walked through the house opening the windows and singing, "Rise and shine and give God your glory, children of the Lord!" My children never saw the night before. I only showed them my tomorrows.

Tomorrows are God's way of telling us that life will go on. It will go on when the days are miserable and it will go on when the days are good. And every opportunity that we have, every moment that our broken hearts beat is another chance.

Buried in the soil of the ordinary, extraordinary does exist.

Funny, in Israel it's not uncommon to see an orthodox Jew standing on the corner in Jerusalem, smoking. The image is paradoxical to us. To them, it's raw; it's honest. Because they understand, they offer no apologies. They gather, thinking and debating the meaning of life through puffs of toxic smoke.

One day, maybe, on a day when it's least expected, we won't smoke anymore. Maybe all of our reasons for smoking will be resolved. Until then, we grieve when grief is required, and we put it away when it's been long enough. Then we go back and do what we came to do in the first place—live.

God heals us, one broken piece, one rare pearl at a time.

The Annual Messianic Weekly Reading Portion

Reading Schedule

*T*his is an introduction to the Annual Messianic Weekly Reading Portion, designed to escort you through the Torah in one year. To fully appreciate the culture of the Weekly Reading Portion you should read according to the traditional Jewish and/or Messianic rhythm. This schedule is posted on all synagogue website calendars and is also readily available to you on my website: www.strengthtozion.com.

I am a Christian.

*Special Readings for Holy Day Observances are excluded from this list.

In The Beginning...	Genesis 1:1 - 6:8	Isaiah 42:5 - 43:11 1 Samuel 20:18-42	John 1:1-14
Noah...	Genesis 6:9 - 11:32	Isaiah 54:1 - 55:5	1 Peter 3:18-22
Go...	Genesis 12:1-17:27	Isaiah 40:27 - 41:16	Romans 4:1-25 Galatians 5:1-6
And Appeared...	Genesis 18:1 - 22:24	2 Kings 4:1-37	2 Peter 2:4-11
Life of Sarah...	Genesis 23:1 - 25:18	1 Kings 1:1-31	1 Corinthians 15:50-57

Generations...	Genesis 25:19 - 28:9	Malachi 1:1 - 2:7	Philippians 2:5-11 Romans 9:6-13
And Went Out...	Genesis 28:10 - 32:3	Hosea 12:13 - 14:10	John 1:43-51
And He Sent	Genesis 32:4 - 36:43	Obadiah 1-21 Hosea 11:7 - 12:12	Matthew 26:36-42
And He Dwelt...	Genesis 37:1 - 40:23	Amos 2:6 - 3:8 Zechariah 3:1 - 4:7 (Hebrew bible Zechariah 2:14 - 4:7)	Acts 7:9-16
At The End...	Genesis 41:1 - 44:17	Zechariah 3:1 - 4:7 (Hebrew bible Zechariah 2:14 - 4:7) 1 Kings 3:15-4:1; 7:40-50	1 Corinthians 2:1-5
And Came Near...	Genesis 44:18 - 47:27	Ezekiel 37:15-28	Luke 6:7-15
And He Lived...	Genesis 47:28 - 50:26	1 Kings 2:1 - 12:1	1 Peter 1:3-9
Names...	Exodus 1:1 - 6:1	Jeremiah 1:1 - 2:3	Acts 7:17-43
And I Appeared...	Exodus 6:2 - 9:35	Ezekiel 28:25 - 29:21	Romans 9:14-21 Hebrews 3:1-6
Come, Go...	Exodus 10:1 - 13:16	Jeremiah 46:13-28	Romans 12:1-8 1 Corinthians 11:20-34
When He Sent...	Exodus 13:17 - 17:16	Judges 4:4 - 5:31	John 6:22-40

Jethro...	Exodus 18:1 - 20:23	Isaiah 6:1 - 7:6, 9:5-6	Matthew 5:17-32 1 Peter 2:4-10
Ordinances...	Exodus 21:1 - 24:18	Jeremiah 34:8-22, 33:25-26 2 Kings 11:17 - 12:17	Matthew 5:17-32 2 Corinthians 6:14-18
Elevation...	Exodus 25:1 - 27:19	1 Kings 5:26 - 6:13	Matthew 5:33-37
You Shall Command...	Exodus 27:20 - 30:10	Ezekiel 43:10-27 1 Samuel 15:1-34	Matthew 5:14-16
When You Take...	Exodus 30:11 - 34:35	1 Kings 18:1-39 Ezekiel 36:16-38	1 Corinthians 8:4-13
And Assembled...	Exodus 35:1 - 38:20	1 Kings 7:13-26, 40-51 Ezekiel 45:16 - 46:18	2 Corinthians 9:6-11
Records/ Accounts...	Exodus 38:21 - 40:38	1 Kings 7:51 - 8:21	2 Corinthians 3:7-18
And He Called...	Leviticus 1:1 - 5:26	1 Samuel 15:1-34 Isaiah 43:21 - 44:23	Hebrews 10:1-18
Command...	Leviticus 6:1 - 8:36	Jeremiah 7:21 - 8:3, 9:22-23 Malachi 3:4-24	Hebrews 8:1-6
Eighth...	Leviticus 9:1 - 11:47	2 Samuel 6:1 - 7:17	Acts 5:1-11, 10:9-22, 34-35
Conceived...	Leviticus 12:1 - 13:59	2 Kings 4:42 - 5:19 Malachi 3:4 - 4:6	Matthew 8:1-4

Infected One...	Leviticus 14:1 - 15:33	2 Kings 7:3-20 Amos 9:7-15	Romans 6:19-23 1 Peter 1:13-16
After Death...	Leviticus 16:1 - 18:30	Amos 9:7-15 Ezekiel 22:1-19	1 Corinthians 6:9-17 Hebrews 9:11-28
Holiness...	Leviticus 19:1 - 20:27	Isaiah 66:1-24 Ezekiel 20:2-20	1 Peter 1:13-16
Say...	Leviticus 21:1 - 24:23	Ezekiel 44:15-31	1 Peter 2:4-10
On The Mount...	Leviticus 25:1 - 26:2	Jeremiah 32:6-27	Luke 4:16-21
In My Instructions...	Leviticus 26:3 - 27:34	Jeremiah 16:19 - 17:14	2 Corinthians 6:14-18 1 Peter 1:13-16
In Wilderness...	Numbers 1:1-4:20	Hosea 2:1-22 1 Samuel 20:18-42	1 Corinthians 12:12-20
Life, Bear Up, Carry, Take...	Numbers 4:21 - 7:89	Judges 13:2-25	Acts 21:17-26
When You Set Up...	Numbers 8:1 - 12:16	Zechariah 2:14 - 4:7	1 Corinthians 10:6-13
Send Forth...	Numbers 13:1 - 15:41	Joshua 2:1-24	Hebrews 3:7-19
Korah...	Numbers 16:1 - 18:32	1 Samuel 11:14 - 12:22	Romans 13:1-7
Statutes...	Numbers 19:1 - 22:1	Judges 11:1-33	1 Corinthians 1:20-31 John 3:10-21

Balak...	Numbers 22:2 - 25:9	Micah 5:6 - 6:8	2 Corinthians 1:20-31
Phineas...	Numbers 25:10-30	1 Kings 18:46 - 19:21	John 2:13-22
Words...	Deuteronomy 1:1 - 3:22	Isaiah 1:1-27	1 Timothy 3:1-7
I Sought...	Deuteronomy 3:23 - 7:11	Isaiah 40:1-26	Mark 12:28-34
Because...	Deuteronomy 7:12 - 11:25	Isaiah 49:14 - 51:3	Romans 8:31-39
Look At, Behold...	Deuteronomy 11:26 - 16:17	Isaiah 54:11 - 55:5	1 John 4:1-6
Judges...	Deuteronomy 16:18 - 21:9	Isaiah 51:12 - 52:12	John 1:19-27 1 Corinthians 5:9-13
When You Go...	Deuteronomy 21:10 - 21:9	Isaiah 54:1-10	Luke 20:27-38 1 Corinthians 5:1-5
When You Come...	Deuteronomy 26:1 - 29:8	Isaiah 60:1-22	Luke 21:1-4 Romans 11:1-15
You are Standing...	Deuteronomy 29:9 - 30:20	Isaiah 61:10 - 63:9 Micah 7:18-20 Joel 2:15-27	Romans 10:1-13 Colossians 3:12-14
And He Went...	Deuteronomy 31:1-30	Isaiah 55:6 - 56:8	Romans 7:7-12
Give Ear...	Deuteronomy 32:1-52	2 Samuel 22:1-51 Hosea 14:2-10	Revelation 15:1-4

| In This Blessing... | Deuteronomy 33:1 - 34:12 | Joshua 1:1-18 | Revelation 21:9 - 22:5 |